By Your Eyes

Briane Willis

To those who persevere.

Chapter 1

The shadows were deep where she crouched, but still the afternoon heat crowded closer. Unlike hair, her crown of snakes didn't stick to her sweaty forehead. Instead, they hissed against Medusa's skin, each thin scaled body growing taut, and her muscles soon did the same.

Something was coming.

She squeezed two handfuls of her aged skirt and squinted, searching for any sign of the unknown threat.

The two dozen living threads on her scalp twisted like ringlets, sinuous waves undulating as if submerged. Then they straightened, preparing to strike an unperceived foe. However unseen to Medusa, that would only be temporary. Her protectors were never wrong.

She rose to peer around the corner of her new home, though to call it that was undeserved. Abandoned for an unknown number of years, the structure was obviously unsound. Out of pure desperation, Medusa had selected this stone pile, sitting flagrantly on the cliff, and crumbling with each gust of wind, as refuge. She should have known better.

But the truth of this place, however doomed or dreary, was a reminder of her own imminent fate.

Flashes of nightmares lodged in her mind, on and off, bright against the darkness of her shuttered lids. His face illuminated with each shuddering slice. His sword glinted, a look of determination cleaving his features. She never outran him in these dreams. He always heralded a particular doom.

Perseus.

She shook herself and strained further, both impatient and dreading any sounds to support the snakes's apprehension, shoving the feelings away. She had to be present to manage what came next. To survive the

1

inevitable.

At last, she detected the squelch of mud, and the following sucking of a shoe tugged free. She swallowed, her breath knotted like brambles.

Has he found me? Even after moving so far away? Her fingers curled into her palm, and moisture gathered in her creased elbow. Her companions lashed out, their tongues flicking for scents and information about the approaching stranger. Then they darted forward with such propulsion that Medusa swayed with them.

"Settle," she said, and they complied minimally.

She had thought this spot was suitable, far enough from the nearby village, secluded. And yet a person had found it. In her experience, people were always dangerous. Regardless of what they said or how they looked, dangerous.

"Woman," the individual said, his voice low. "I haven't seen you before. Where do you come from?"

Body prickling in multiple limbs at once, she pressed a hand over her mouth. She understood immediately. He hadn't seen her snakes, nor had he heard the rumors that sprouted in her wake. To him, she was a normal woman to covet and claim.

Medusa took a quiet breath and gripped her knife until her fingers turned white. Needle sharpness arrived soon after, but she didn't notice. All that mattered was the potential attacker, the threat. Her companions slithered and coiled above her, hungry to destroy him.

She forced herself to calm the vibration of fear swirling through her and prepared her iciest tone. "Begone from here. You're not welcome."

The footsteps paused, followed by the dry clearing of a throat.

"This place is unclaimed," he said. "None to say I can't walk here. Nothing you can do about it, in fact."

Medusa's stomach soured at the confidence of his delivery, guessing he was a man rarely questioned in his life. Never reduced to an object. He was someone with power.

A chorus of hisses flowed in response. She inched higher to peek through the broken window, the idea that such a house offered safety feeling increasingly foolish.

She couldn't stay here, not now, so easily discovered a few days into her residence. She had chosen the wrong area to settle, and such a mistake could cost her everything.

Whoever he was, he remained out of sight, taking measured paces as if circling prey.

"I saw you arrive. This place isn't suited for you. It's much too brutal." He paused before speaking again. "I can protect you, keep you safe in this world. You would consider it a gift, my companionship."

Something black and viscous seemed to drip from his words as he spoke. She knew what he came for. What Poseidon had come for.

Possession. Control.

Horror wrapped up her spine, twisting her lungs and squeezing her thoughts. But that was momentary, a reaction of pure memory. Next came the onslaught of rage to mimic the sea thrashing the rocks below the cliff.

The snakes swarmed, bodies whipping. *I'm not alone.* She would show him how wrong he was.

"You will never tell anyone of my strength," she said, imbuing the statement with every ounce of her vitriol. "Or the company I keep."

In a flurry of determination and serpentine urgency, she straightened and rushed around the corner of the house. He jerked at her sudden appearance, taking a step backward. His gaze tripped over her worn shirt, weathered skirt, and he blinked. His tawny complexion paled as his lips parted.

"You're a monster," he said, both arms wrenched upward, as if to cover his face.

But it was too late.

The stonification started at his pupils, a grayness that spiraled out to his brows, nose, and jowls. Next were his ears and hair, then his lips, frozen in a gaping circle. His tongue hardened in the cavern of his mouth, the tendons like ropes beneath his deadened skin. The twitches of his panic stilled after several long seconds, as she watched it all unfold.

It was no longer than a few seconds before his flesh fully transformed to polished rock.

He stood beside her front door, rooted to the spot, observing his upper half, which reared back from the change. He had known terror at the end, just as Medusa had known terror, and he wouldn't hurt anyone else again. No more women or animals broken in his arrogance.

Good riddance, she thought.

The victory was short-lived, her pulse quickening with the realization some might come looking for him.

How lucky if he has people who love him.

She once had such individuals, ones who loved her, but no family members sought her after the attack. She had knelt in Athena's temple, battered from her skin to her soul. No part had survived unscathed and no part had healed. Even the scars from trying to escape him would forever adorn her body.

Her hand flew to the weak wall, finding support as the hot, sharpened memory slashed deeper. Bile rising, she tried swallowing, and grimaced at the failure.

Wind darted through the narrow passage between the man's statued arm and torso, whistling, and she startled. She swayed on her feet, the impression her bare toes in the cool dirt too much. The serpents by her temples nestled close, reminding her of where she was, that they were present.

Unlike what that man had said, she wasn't alone.

Her crowd of snakes had appeared as she curled into herself after Poseidon's assault. Her guardians, companions. The only family that remained.

Tiny tongues flicked her cheekbones, and she inclined her head at the pressure. She had to do this.

Despite how long it would take, Medusa began to push.

***

The man's statue splintered raucously, erupting into a heap on the beach below. She wiped her hands and stilled her trembling limbs, transfixed by the shade of the statue's inner stone. She had no idea why such a difference existed between the outside and inside stone's hue. Perhaps there was no reason, though she knew the exterior changed depending on the person.

You should have left. You didn't have to die, pathetic man.

She rubbed her arms, the frigid salty mist more taunt that relief, while the surging wind stuck her clothes stiff against her body.

The horde of snakes rippled, spitting down at the man's remains. She hated how, even now, she questioned what that man's intentions were.

The stranger might have been earnest in his search for a partner. Someone to love. And isn't that a noble pursuit?

Then she remembered his words, his tone, how violently the snakes turned at his abrupt approach. No, coming after her wasn't noble, and she had warned him. He came anyway and she wouldn't mourn the dead, hardened thing he became.

He joined many others who had disturbed her life, dozens who mistakenly looked at her. Each of those men were broken statues scattered across the landscape, save for the worst of them, who claimed godliness. He was first and most despicable, who had escaped justice and likely wrought further violence whenever possible.

Medusa glanced over the cliff once more, soothing a snake by her earlobe. It curled up the shell of her ear, the silky flow of its scales relaxing her. Below them, a familiar tumult churned; sand, shell, and stone slowly, effortlessly, crushed by the weight of waves.

Her breath gradually evened, but her heart continued its pronounced rhythm. There was nothing of the attacker alive at the cliff's base. Still, risk doused the air. She would be extra cautious at all times, and hope no one else saw her arrive.

With a glance at the sky, she noted the waning afternoon hour, and walked inside to retrieve her bag. It was too soon. She needed food, and only days after depleting her reserves traveling to this doomed cliff. Several recognizable plants grew at the edge of the forest she'd seen. Tangy blossoms. Seed that filled a belly. A snake by her chin twined along her finger, which rested under her chin. This was a comforting, if unconscious, habit, and her frown lifted further.

They set off, Gorgon and her crowd of serpents, toward the forest, the multitude of heads darting around them for any signs of another person approaching. Fresh clouds ate up the sky, gray and heavy, as if carrying more than moisture. Medusa wrinkled her nose at the additional constraint on time and walked as fast as she deemed reasonable.

She left the hilly plain, and trees consumed her in silence, their living cathedral more welcoming than any structure she'd ever encountered. Flowers in soft shades of yellows and pinks to deep purple hues clumped in patches of sunlight. Vines draped from branches, plants that lived off light, the canopy allowed entrance. Thick, lush ferns draped around trunks, and she almost smiled at the visual effect of clothing. If this forest was dressed for anything, it was spring, however prompt summer was this year.

She almost smiled, forgetting the recent confrontation and resulting death for a just a moment. Here she was in a home she might have loved.

Despite living most of her youth on a small island and staying close ever since, she wanted a break from the ocean. Its relentless tug and melancholy temperance clung to her. Incapable of returning to her family, she fought against the cloying shame that made her chest constrict. But her gaze always found the ocean. Better to see Poseidon coming, to prepare to fight him off if he dared violate her a second time.

More than anything, Medusa understood, beneath the layers of skin and emotion, she hadn't let go of the past.

Or perhaps it's the past that holds onto me.

She swallowed the usual acrid taste that accompanied memories. It always stung. Perhaps it always would.

She straightened to release the melancholic thoughts, and the snakes tickled her cheeks. In unison, her living halo and her eyes leapt to a deer nearby who has raised its head, spooked by her deliberately quiet steps, but quickly eased by her presence. She crouched to pluck several brown and white mushrooms, plus a handful of clover seedpods. They were small but packed with flavor and a satisfying snack. Some sorrel caught her attention next, and she nestled her harvest in the leather bag strapped across her torso.

In an hour, she found a sufficient amount of food to last her several days. Since she was on the western region, she walked closer to the edge, the side closest to the human village, to be certain that no one followed. It was better to confront fear rather than run from it, after all.

She knew the man's footsteps would be drying from his trek earlier that day. What she didn't expect was a fresh set near the first tracks. She gulped a gasp, which hardened in her belly, and studied the direction the impressions went.

The second trail ran parallel to the first, steps uneven but unwavering. And they pointed directly toward her valley.

Chapter 2

She crept along the forest gloom for an hour, tracking the footprints as they crossed the land. Thunder rumbled with increasing frequency, and she instinctively gathered dry, fallen branches for a fire. She hated the rain, hated that kind of vulnerability. A fire would be an additional risk, but it was logical to be prepared, all the same.

Her snakes conveyed their unease by a fierce twisting of bodies. They wouldn't fail her, neither would her murderous sight, but they preferred to avoid confrontations altogether. Medusa exhaled soft noises, a lullaby of whispers, until each one drifted closer to her scalp once more.

We need to sneak up on this person, she thought at them. As if hearing her response, the reptiles subdued, but none grew less observant.

She paused at the edge of the forest. Her arms ached from the clutch of wood, making her shift their positioning. A swath of clouds eclipsed the declining sun and evening unspooled around them, unconcerned with their insecurity. Still, she traced the lines of footprints, unable to decipher which was the original attacker. If these two worked together, there was no obvious reason why they traveled in such a way. And worse, if there was a companion, they would pursue their friend more deliberately than at a distance, she reasoned.

The gentle slope shifted wider between the hills, which Medusa hadn't yet explored. Several tall trees dotted the gentle valley, and a vivid shade of green decorated the land. This region boasted more rainfall than her previous location. A creek in the forest poured a river and scampered toward the coast.

She hadn't been able to wash yet, despite how much she craved it. There was quite a list of duties required that her attention before such an indulgence, including shoring up the crumbling house and finding food.

Her eyes scraped the scene, searching for any signs of people. Strangely, the trails diverged. One shifted to the river, rather than the coast. *Perhaps the two aren't together after all,* she thought.

She stayed low, nibbling the flesh of her inner cheek. With narrowed eyes, she detected a smear of brown against the grass in the distance. In shock, her bundle of logs fell, and she darted behind a lone tree growing beyond the forest's edge. Then she heard curious notes drifting over the landscape.

With a frown, she leaned toward the sound, hoping to glean a tune. A voice came next, low and harmonic, skilled in swinging between notes. She shuttered her lids and listened harder over what appeared to be an encroaching storm.

At the first words, her jaw dropped, and the snakes sparked into a circle of fear.

"It can't be," she whispered. But the refrain repeated, of snakes and great beauty, of a gaze that promised death. Of a solitary creature cursed in body, mind, and spirit.

The singer repeated one word in particular.

"Medusa." The voice reached her like a plague. *"Medusa."*

***

Her skirt twisted at her knees, bunched in her bloodless knuckles as she ran. Breath came in jagged spurts, the remnants of a final gasp that likely wouldn't last her sprint home. She hoped it wasn't too late, that he hadn't seen her, that she had enough of a lead.

It was the man from her nightmares. The hero Perseus sent by the gods to kill her, destroy whatever was left of her after Poseidon's attack.

The lopsided tombstone shaped structure loomed ahead, and she sprinted through the unhinged door. Dread returned with force, slamming into her chest, and sending ripples of tension through hr limbs.

She had to get away before he found her. After her many months seeking somewhere safe, this pathetic hovel wouldn't house her even a few days, the shortest residence yet.

He won't find us, she thought. *He won't kill us.* The snakes hissed their conviction.

Medusa grabbed her larger leather satchel and spare clothes. The items landed in the satchel, layered on top of her foraging bag, and both bounced as she raced around the old house. Her canteen was woefully empty by then.

I'll have to stop by the river before I go east, she thought. It was a dangerous prospect, but unavoidable. All she could hope for was this new threat to be nowhere nearby as he planned her demise.

So many others had failed to destroy her. She refused to let this person change that, no matter how long she would have to flee.

A bird shrieked overhead, startling Medusa and her snakes as they exited the crooked-hanging door. Her sinuous aura hissed, arching upward, then settled at the sight of the bird. But their lithe forms kept a taut energy, ready to strike any possible attacker.

Once, Medusa loathed what Athena had foisted upon her, an added insult to Poseidon's injury. The new sensation was of constant moving, roiling, shuddering across her scalp. The creatures were at first deeply foreign, yet entwined. Worse, the snakes seemed a continuation of her violation. She had not agreed to it, had only woken to her new state of existence, forced to accept the replacement of her hair with living, writhing beings.

Now, however, she couldn't imagine life without them.

Medusa clutched her canteen to as she moved toward the river. She regretted not having gone fishing the previous day. The lack of fish would be a hurdle unless she stuck close to the coastline. An image of a boat materialized in her mind, and sailing far away from this place. She would have to abandon this land entirely.

The rumble of the river announced their proximity. She held her breath and peered around, pausing in the direction where she spotted the singing man. There was no one as far as she could see. She resumed her pace, shoed feet making no noise in the early night.

Only then did the river come into clear view, and a dense form hunched at its bank.

She collapsed to the ground and crawled, dropping her canteen and wishing there was time to soothe her snakes. Though fearful, they prepared for attack, ever her dutiful guardians. In silence, they watched the man retrieve his own water from the cool crystalline waters.

By all estimation, he hadn't recognized her approach.

He wore a white shirt, baggy and stained, and too small. The muddied trousers clung to him and she noticed spray from the river glistening on his arms. He raised the water to his mouth and drank deeply, slowly, and she furrowed her brow. This man showed none of the behaviors honed by a hunter. There was an ease about him, not necessarily confidence or assurance, but a speed of movement that made her feel he had nothing else. As if coming after her was his sole option.

His head turned and in the last of daylight, she saw his profile, so unlike what she saw in the terror of her dreams. His nose was large, smooth, unlike the one affixing Perseus's more traditionally chiseled face.

Something in his shifting entranced her. There was a difference in his body, how his head didn't turn with the rest of him, like his eyes didn't lead his actions.

She ground her teeth until the pressure ached. The man filled his canteen again and stood, his head swiveling to either side. Her snakes chirped angrily, a chorus of tiny sounds she feared drifted to him. She pressed her palms over them, and they obeyed, quieting under her pressure.

But the damage was done.

"I know you're there," the man said.

Medusa winced, inching backward on the grass. His next words froze her in place.

"I mean you no harm. I am aware of the stories and I do not come here to die by your power."

She crouched, frozen for some time, then snuck to her vantage point, revealing the top half of her head. His weight moved between his legs as the canteen swayed at his wrist, hands up in surrender. Each second she delayed the snakes grew more frenzied, jostling in a swarm of distress.

To her wonder, he stuck an arm behind him without turning his face, and brought forth his instrument.

"I know what the gods did to you. They took something from you, as they did from me. I know why you hurt others and I don't judge you for it." His tone shook like the thunder in an approaching cloud. "I admire you."

He sat down, knees jutting out as he folded himself into a seated position, and began strumming.

"I wrote a song about you." There was a tremor in his voice. "About how you've triumphed. I will play it if you will listen." His dark curls fell onto his forehead, a pattern like burnt straw in the wind.

She wished something about him made sense.

Every part of her yelled, a rising tide of dread. She knew she should leave, find another water source, never look back. He held no obvious weapons, reclined in a position that would be difficult to leap from quickly. And there was that unique way his eyes remained still.

Ignoring the drum of her snakes in protest against her scalp, she rose from her hiding place, and took one nervous step at a time. He waited, playing a tune on the strings that was barely audible. He was a stranger, holding no resemblance to the glinting hero of her nightmares, and referencing her exploits.

It was worth a small risk, be concluded.

A small smile transformed the man's mouth as she neared.

"Hello, Medusa."

She said nothing while her snakes hissed. He turned toward her, face tilted to hers. Her heart seized, but he did not transform. His skin retained its color, like ripe apricots, and his limbs flowed in all of their human strength.

Her confusion wound itself into a knot, followed by understanding that seemed to arrive much too late.

He is blind.

Chapter 3

"I understand if you're afraid."

Medusa stiffened, frowned, bounced between her feet. To flee was the most obvious path. Instead, she studied his features. The river separating them eased her nerves, but she was no less affronted by his presumption.

"You can't claim to know me," she said, as a lightning strike flashed.

"That's true." The murmur of his deep breath drifted to her. "I've been afraid."

A lull of silence drifted, filled only by thunder. It was an invitation he left for her. She failed to ignore it.

"Why?"

He shrugged, as if his own fear was mundane as mud on his shoe. "The gods took my sight, and they may take further pieces of me. I have learned to live without sight, but I'm not sure I would overcome such a loss again."

She stepped to the water's edge, desperate to hear him over the river's incessant gurgling.

"Why did they blind you?"

He set his instrument down, flexing his open hands. "I can only guess, but they might have believed I gazed upon the world with too much curiosity."

"They are the arrogant ones." Her snakes spat alongside her words.

"Ah. You are brave—or reckless—to say so. Perhaps both. Whatever the case, your defiance is why I am here."

She tilted her head, and her companions mimicked the movement. The man's chin hung on his chest. He was immune to her supposed beauty, and though he sang of it, there was no reason to direct his face to her.

The possibility of his claim being true made her sway. That he came out of admiration and reverence, a more enticing reason than the ones of which haunted her. And beyond that, her power was useless against him. He was impervious to her particularly gruesome punishment.

Strangely, even if he wasn't, she loathed the prospect of turning him to stone.

The realization landed with such disorienting force she spun on her heels, bounded up the hill, and left him where he stood, cleaved in shadow and a bright flare of lightning.

***

The door refused to shut.

There was little point in pushing it into the frame, since the walls had several oddly shaped holes, and the remaining stones threatened to fall at any moment.

Medusa leaned against the splintering wood, breath going in and out quick enough to leave her light-headed. Her snakes lapped gently, attempting to counter the stress of all that unfolded, and she nuzzled them in return.

Will he risk crossing the river? His blindness was a defense against her, but a hindrance in many more ways, she guessed. To imagine living in the world in darkness, and after experiencing the light, plucked a chill from her spine.

But it wasn't so different from her own loss. Instinctively, she hugged herself.

She once took her connection to those she loved for granted. Now, her family was lost to her because of shame and fear. No longer to sing with her sisters, tell stories, or feast together. The gods stole light from her life, too.

Medusa steadied herself and forced a confidence to her steps she didn't feel. She shook with hunger, thirst, and distress. As she realized her canteen remained where it was, she grunted sharply.

All reason seemed to have left her upon meeting this man. She mulled over the details, calculating, considering.

The threat he posed began to diminish. After all, this man wasn't reminiscent of the terror of her nightmares, nor did he look particularly honed for battle. Though large in stature, his muscles didn't have the striking delineation of others who came to kill her.

No, there was a chance this man spoke the truth.

Still, she wavered. It would be an interesting approach, presenting themself as non-threatening, until she let her guard down. Then, he would strike.

She pinched the bridge of her nose, ignoring the tug of thirst, and focused on her heartbeat. She needed to reclaim rationality, to prioritize a path of survival.

Water was urgent, especially if she was to escape. That was the first task.

But that would entail returning to the river, and her previous attempt hadn't gone well.

Descend the cliff, she thought suddenly. The path was quite vertical and the man likely wouldn't dare pursue her, let alone find it. She could stay in the crags, watching the cliff side above, waiting to see if he came after her. But it was nighttime, and she was reluctant to taunt death by falling.

Anything was better than staying in the crumbling structure. She needed to be decisive, needed to choose.

To dismiss the muddled confusion would unveil curiosity, she knew, an undeniable pull toward him. Or didn't want to.

Then a whirl of storm winds arrived, leaving her more frazzled than before.

She stomped once, making her decision. She would run to gather her canteen, then climb down the cliff face during nighttime, for she trusted her feet. That was, if he didn't remain at the river, waiting for her. Playing a song about her exploits.

Heat rose in her cheeks, a baffling reaction to the silliness of a melody played by a stranger. It didn't stop until the blush infiltrated her neck, collar bones, down the more-pale skin of her chest.

Tiny tongues struck her forehead as if in warning. Medusa intuitively understood it wasn't about physical danger, but something far more abstract. Something emotional.

With a quick nod, she departed the structure and rushed back to the river, cursing herself for leaving the canteen. Her heavy bag thumped on her thigh, a rhythm that increased her confidence. She could do this, would survive another man.

When she neared the river, her eyes caught on a fire. A tent stood nearby, a dark figure hunched over something. She caught the lilt of his instrument once more.

Did he steal my firewood? But she noticed her discarded pile farther to the right. His fire would die soon, she realized. Raindrops fell in small handfuls.

He had moved closer to the river, yet he remained a fair distance away. His back was to her, a sign of privacy, she guessed. Or a trick.

Over the crackle of his fire and song, she doubted her approach was audible. But she crept slowly, cautiously, down the gentle decline. Her canteen sat where she dropped it by a large, sun-bleached rock. She grasped it, her attention focused on the man in the near distance, and wrinkled her brow. The container was full.

Did he fill it after I left? The two snakes closest to her temples turned rigid at the possibility. She patted them each and poured out the water in case of poisoning. *Better to be safe and spend several more seconds refilling the container than dead,* she thought.

A voice split the quiet, and she jolted, fingers loosening on her canteen. She snatched it up before the river swept it away.

"Would you care for some dinner?"

She straightened, fastened the top on her water, and took a step back. To her dismay, a rumble sounded in her stomach. She pressed a hand to stifle it and forced out a low, firm voice.

"No. I don't know you and I don't want to."

The fire illuminated his profile, outlining his strong nose and brow once more. She noted how his lips opened and closed, signaling a chewing of words, but rather than release them, he simply nodded. As he returned his focus to the fire in front of him, Medusa's heart sank.

I wish I could say yes.

"I'll leave in the morning, then." A different tone accompanied his statement, melancholy and layered.

Once more, her heartbeat faltered.

Wait, she urged herself to say.

Instead, she asked, "Where do you come from?"

"The town beside the forest. I'm Leandros. Since I know your name, it's only fair to share mine." He audibly sniffed the air. "Would you like to get out of the oncoming storm?"

She ignored his question and the slowly quickening drops. "How did you sense I would be here?"

He adjusted his hold on the instrument and said, "I can't really explain it. A man said he saw a woman alone, moving into an old house by the cliffs. He bragged, said horrible things..." The man, Leandros, straightened. "When he didn't come back, I followed."

15

"Is it possible others followed?" She pulled her bottom lip between her teeth.

"It is possible. He did have a brother."

Anxiety sliced her, and she swayed on her feet. "I don't understand."

"About brothers?" He cracked the smallest of smiles.

"No," she said with a sharp exhale. "Why are you here at all?"

"Oh. Well." He paused again and stirred the bubbling soup. "I've been a lonely person for most my life. I thought I'd try reaching out to some other lonely person. Maybe we wouldn't have to be that way anymore."

She blinked, unsure if she heard him right. No one had said such things to her in many years. She frowned, her blood pumping too hard in her fingertips. Her snakes braided themselves, coiling into thick veins, their faces packed closely as if conferring on the matter. She didn't blame them; his sincerity couldn't possibly be true and required suspicion.

Still, his head fell in the onrushing silence.

Have I been lonely? Anger followed his unexpected suggestion, that he could claim she needed anyone. *No,* she thought, *he's a fool to think he knows me.* But even as she concluded this, the prickles of her rage subsided.

She stared at him, willing him to speak, while he seemed to wait for her response.

Rain fell hard all at once, thick and frigid, and she grimaced up at the black sky. It would be a long storm, she guessed, and the resulting flood would scour everything, from trees firmly rooted to the soil itself. His humble tent and fire would be destroyed.

Perhaps it's for the best he leaves soon, she reasoned.

The snakes tangled around her ears, their myriad huffs reaching for language they would never grasp. But she understood them. She always would.

"Don't stay the night," she said.

He flinched as if she'd thrown scalding liquid at him.

"I mean..." She floundered for a softer explanation. "This storm will be wild. You should find shelter somewhere before it's too late."

He inclined his face, lids closing, and for a moment he seemed to relish the upsurge of wind.

"You're right," he said, and rose to his feet.

To collapse his camp required a few minutes, but already she sensed how he would take longer without the use of his eyes. He appeared to ignore her then, focusing on his task. The smell of his soup ribboned on the gusts, and her mouth watered.

She clenched her fists as an image solidified in her mind, of inviting him to her pathetic house, of enjoying the warm soup together, huddled in the only dry section of the ancient building.

The fantasy was almost comforting, almost tempting.

"No, that's not possible." Her words escaped beneath her breath, and the snakes swam in agreement. There had been no trustworthy man before this one, and nothing had changed.

She turned, already shivering from the rain, and hurried away.

"Goodbye, Medusa," he called.

He sent the farewell over his shoulder, voice seemingly snagging on the rough fibers of his shirt.

Her teeth ground, bit her tongue. Caused a multitude of physical distractions. His farewell elicited a fluttering sensation. But she didn't look back.

Chapter 4

The storm raged for a day, releasing walls of driving rain without end.

Clouds swirled murky as cold pools at high tide. Medusa's snakes hung low, energy depleted for mysterious reasons. Perhaps they reflected her own state--soggy, regretful.

She wondered if Leandros had left, found higher ground, had wanted to stay. To cast him off with distrust was to douse a fledgling hope inside her.

That after all these years, perhaps she wasn't destined to be alone.

Impossible. Self-loathing hardened in its place.

To her embarrassment, she wondered how that song sounded. How his voice would have sculpted her name as music, echoing between the walls of her house as they waited out the deluge.

She hadn't left the crumbling structure, though she tried at dawn and in the afternoon. Reasons to stay crowded together, like invisible hurdles—that few were foolish enough to come look for her in this dangerous weather, to keep herself healthy. After all, her snakes disliked being wet more than she did. And if they grew sick, as they had upon occasion, she suffered more from the illness.

A single reason pulsed beneath the others. *Leandros is still here and he might need help.*

Earlier that day, just for a moment, a flimsy clutch of seconds, she swore the wind had delivered his voice. Sadness followed, her expression sunk, stomach churned. She needed a distraction. She needed food.

As she made her way down the cliff in the deluge, a rock slipped beneath her foot, and she lurched to the side, snakes thrashing helplessly. She caught herself, both hands flying at the rock wall and crouching on the narrow path. Other loose bits fell, smashing to smaller fractured pieces on the beach below. The snakes shivered, a swarm of dejection. With hands clutched at her chest, she listened to them untangle themselves, stabilizing herself once more. Two seemed genuinely frustrated by the near catastrophe, while others comforted her. In the interim, her stomach grumbled, and the aroma of Leandros's soup was only a taunt of memory.

If only I had said yes.

Regardless of what form her thoughts took, hunger wouldn't wait.

She gingerly hopped the remaining path onto solid ground, drenched to her very bones. Her feet shifted to disperse her weight, the sharp outcroppings resistant to the crash of waves nearby. To linger here would be careless. The priority was catching fish and getting away soon, for her delay was already extensive, and fear edging her every movement.

A tidal pool nestled on the southern strip of the beach where the ocean suddenly deepened, allowing more fish congregated. She'd discovered this helpful, natural hunting pool when initially she looked down at the beach. It was a primary reason for choosing this place.

Now, she pulled her soaking shirt from sticking to her skin and spread old berries into the pool. Unperturbed by the storm above, the fish promptly burst to the surface, and she snagged them with her hand-stitched net. This approach required patience and a steady arm, and she had perfected both. The waves swept in and kicked up a frigid froth, casting her in an additional layer of chill. Only two days prior she had complained of unseasonable heat.

She bit her lip and caught a third, fourth, fifth fish. They plopped onto the ground, where she killed them quickly with a strike to the head. Her snakes nearly whined their protest, hungry but waterlogged. They hated most forms of water, which colored their proximity to the sea as rather tragic in Medusa's estimation.

And yet there was a deeper tragedy between them and the ocean, of course.

Despite Poseidon's forever threat looming in the darkened waves, she remained beside the sea, no matter where she went. She faced her fear on the brink of land and liquid, searching for her prior youthful defiance, a trait that had been scrubbed from her two years previously.

You will not break me as you break water upon land. I am stronger than you know.

More thunder rattled the sky, and her halo swirled like sea grass. Soon, the chill would turn to illness, likely immobilizing her with coughs for days, and her travel preparations were far from complete.

Her submerged net filled with fish seeking the berries. Though her legs ached from her perch, she kept her body frozen. She had to be patient, for pulling up too soon would scare away the fish.

At last, the rest of the fish she needed congregated, their silver-grey bodies blending into the cold water, and she snatched up the woven net. Water bounced off the flapping bodies that protested leaving their sanctuary, and large drops were flung from the fibers. She gathered the several rounds of dead fish, clasped the net closed, and sprinted the rocky beach to the path. The bundle bounced against her back, growing heavier from the rain, but she scampered up the cliff as hastily as she dared.

This would last her several days, in case the storm lingered. She'd never smoked her catch indoors before, but the structure she called home hardly qualified as indoors. The smell would infiltrate her clothes, but the fire might also dry her. It was a worthy calculation to prepare for her upcoming departure.

A fleeting vision of sharing the preserved fish with Leandros sent a jolt through her, a seizing of emotion and risk. The sky above followed, a coincidental mimicry that elicited an uncomfortable squeeze in her chest.

She kept climbing.

***

The small pile of stone released a steady stream of smoke that pitched toward the nearest window frame. Usually, she would exercise caution with the volume of smoke required for her task. But the rain covered it well enough, dispersing the smoke so none would be drawn to it in the unlikely event they wandered in the storm.

She couldn't tell if Leandros would search for her. She couldn't admit why she almost wanted him to.

As the snakes napped, lulled by the warmth of the rocks, Medusa cleansed the fish oil for soap. It wasn't ideal, but she didn't dare visit town to purchase a superior oil, not after a neighbor had gone missing.

She had made soap since childhood, infused with flowers whenever possible, and now found gratitude for any cleanliness in all its forms. Never in her childhood days did she crave it. Not until the attack, and after, she didn't feel clean for years.

Her sisters Stheno and Euryale first showed Medusa the process of soak making. She'd considered it a silly pastime, an activity not worth her attention. Of course, theirs had been far more beautiful and finer smelling, but her own soaps were effective enough.

If only my sister could understood how thankful I am.

Medusa stoked the fire with a stick jabbed between the stones, shifting the fish pieces wrapped in large leaves from the forest, and worked her lips. An idea formed like a body in the fishy haze. She let it take shape instead of shoving it away.

Soap is a good trade, and the blind man might need some. She could be persuasive, if she tried, and the hope he would accept stoked brighter. It would be a fine barter, she decided, for a batch of his soup. He'd seemed genuine in his offer, and that was a rare thing indeed.

Better still, a chance to rest in his tent gleamed, a tantalizing prospect. She wouldn't complain if he sang, strummed his instrument, told her more of his defiance of the gods. The imagery was cozy, comforting, and oddly irresistible.

Action seized her limbs, and she jerked upright, her snakes jostling awake to mewl unhappily. She gave them a round of apologetic taps and prepared for her trip to the river. First she doused the fire, moved the rocks, and let the leaf parcels cool. Rain still thrashed the small building, but she had braved worse before.

I just hope he's there.

She removed the heated fish with another few layers of leaves, unwrapped the meat, and nestled them into pots for later eating. She set aside the soap, eager for it to set. Lightning flicked through the plum-hued clouds, startling her, but set her direction with a firm nod.

She clutched a stretch of canvas as a jacket and lurched outside. The rain came so fast and thick she considered calling her movement through it swimming. But this wasn't as uncomfortable as the loose stitch of Leandros disrupting her day. Better to know if he's here or gone, she concluded.

This trek was less dangerous than her scramble down the cliff. Everything felt muffled, and more than once she darted a frenzied look around, fearing a stranger. But she saw none. She held the soaking canvas at her throat and pushed on into the growing gloom of night.

The river was louder than it had been two days prior after the rain had fallen upriver of the village. Water had to flow, and flow it did. She stopped, searched, shivered.

The water exceeded the banks and submerged whatever might have remained of his camp.

Frustration scratched at her. *This is my fault,* she thought. *I shouldn't have left him.*

Voices whirled nearby, making Medusa freeze. Even her lungs paused mid-breath. She ignored how the rain unfurled in cold, heavy sheets. Each snake on her scalp writhed, their recent warmth lost. None of that mattered, as her blood thickened in her veins.

The voices rose over the rainfall's din.

She clambered along the bank heading upriver, unable to cross because of the rising levels, and aggrieved by her slow pace. The voices sounded close, yet there was no sign of anyone. Her legs cramped, a stitch developed in her side. He had only just entered her life and the prospect of his absence was more profoundly concerning that the threat of a lightning strike.

Is there anyone else like him, with his songs and soup, and kindness? Her teeth rattled.

The next strike of lightning reflected off two men on the opposite bank, throwing fists at the other. One of them shouted into the thickening darkness of the storm.

"Where is she?"

"You'll never find her. I promise you that," the taller man said.

Medusa froze, ears straining, and realized the second man was Leandros. He grappled with the sighted man despite his obvious wounds. A wet blotch of red stained the color of Leandros's shirt. Rainfall dragged the crimson hue from the cuts on his face, mingling his life-force with the deadened fabric below.

He was still here. She didn't have the clarity to consider why.

"Leandros!" she screamed.

The two men spun in her direction, mouths open. Leandros stepped forward, angling past the shorter man, but stopped at the sound of the river.

"You have to go hide!" he shouted.

The other man shoved him aside and darted closer to the swelling bank, his snarl flashing in the rain.

"You! Murderous witch! My brother is missing. You killed him, didn't you?"

Medusa stepped back, one hand gripping the top of her drenched shirt. The snakes gave their full frightening display, making the man pause. It was too dark. He couldn't fully perceive her.

"What… What is that?" He gaped, frowned, swiped at his lip. "You're worse than a witch. You're… a monster."

"He came to hurt me," she said too quietly. She conjured more volume and shrieked, "I told him to leave me alone!"

"I can hardly believe that," the man said, voice splintered with pain. The storm made the air too thick.

Leandros balled his fists. "She isn't a monster. Your brother was."

Eyebrows creasing, Medusa glanced at Leandros. He couldn't have known that, but still he spoke with certainty.

"I'll destroy you," the man said to her, seemingly not hearing Leandros. "I'll rip you apart for what you did!"

Medusa shook her head. The dead brother's statue face flashed on her shuttered lids, his terror rippling through his stuck expression. Fear was his last feeling. And now it would be hers.

"I'm coming to get you, little monster," the man said, stepping toward the swelling river. "I'll cross this. I'll cross whatever I have to. You won't kill anyone else."

She turned and ran, her muscles tensed and sore, mind a miasma of distress. This had happened before, and she barely escaped. Luck could only get her so far.

The last thing she heard was a loud yelp that was devoured by the raucous surroundings. She risked a glance over her shoulder, and the bank was empty of anyone. Not the dead man's brother. Not Leandros.

Both had disappeared into the roaring mass of water.

Chapter 5

Gone. Lost. Drowned.

Medusa forced her lungs to expand, palms pressed together by her nose. The whirl of snakes stopped hissing, stopped moving altogether. Despite the torrential downpour, they matched her misery. It swathed her entire being.

Leandros pushed that man, got rid of him for me, she realized. *He attacked him to protect me.*

Medusa stared at the spot where both men had stood seconds ago, incapable of comprehending the facts before her. The gray-black water churned in the darkness, upon itself, and upward, but most of all, crashing down the hill. It devoured the gentle valley with a single, elongated bite.

So too had it eaten Leandros.

Their interaction wasn't meant to unfold as chaos and separation. This was supposed to be her chance to offer a gift, to give him a chance —herself a chance—when earlier she couldn't consider anything beyond rejection. Every aspect of her life had inverted over the two days since their initial meeting, and the truth left her buzzing. Wrecked.

She dropped to her knees and rocked in the soppy grass, ringlets of snakes swinging with each movement. They persisted in their maladroit writhing, but she found no secret reserve of energy sufficient to rise herself. If death lingered close because of rain and chill, she didn't care. There was finally a person who chose her, who sought her not for murder nor possession, and she had banished him to certain death.

Just as she had every man who looked at her since Athena's curse of isolation. Her gift of protection.

Since Medusa discovered Leandros's blindness, a belief formed at the furthest edge of her consciousness that he would be different. Perhaps that she, too, could be different.

She'd denounced him immediately, not because he aimed to destroy her, but because the alternative prospect was unfathomable.

With a lurch that seemed to originate outside herself, she scrambled downriver, remaining near the top of the hill, and scoured the turbid flow. White bubbles frothed at the surface, and she caught herself before tumbling into its depths. Debris slipped past in the tortuous raging water, branches and trunks merely jagged parts of the whole.

Leandros inhabited her thoughts, a light to guide her, a purpose to pursue.

Please say you're holding onto a tree, she thought, nails cutting in her palms.

But even with something to help him keep afloat, doubt curdled in her at once. *Who could survive this?* The other man was now wholly irrelevant. She imagined what it might mean if he miraculously survived, and dismissed the prospect. Her objective was Leandros.

She grabbed her fraying skirt and stumbled to the river's edge.

***

At night, floodwaters were even more dangerous.

The roar to her left increased, the rain kept its shocking pace, and the ground grew steadily more saturated. She lost one old sandal in the muddied grass but kept running, ignoring the ache in her toes. It wouldn't be long before she was numb all over.

That was irrelevant. Her continued refrain pelted as she hurried, *find Leandros alive and safe, locate shelter.* Her determination hadn't failed her ever before, no matter the wounds of body, heart, or mind she endured. And now, knowing what he had done for her, she would return his gift with proper gratitude.

As she ran parallel to the coastline, the river cutting its way toward the lowest point with staggering haste, another awareness struck harder than the torrents of rain.

He might have already been dragged out of reach, and hurtled into the ocean. Even if he survived the journey, he probably wouldn't survive being spat into the gelid nighttime waves.

She forced her legs faster, shuddering, shallow gasps copying the staccato of her heart. If saving Leandros meant saving the man bent on hurting her, she decided she would do it. Anything to make sure the strangely kind, selfless, earnest human who apparently witnessed her beyond the ability of sight would survive.

A strike of lightning tore the sky into fragments for an instant. The illumination caught on a shape beside the river, the bottom half submerged. Medusa yelped, tripped, rolled toward it. *It might be the brother,* she thought, and her snakes bared themselves for battle.

As the level rose to consume him, she grasped his hand frantically to pull him out of the river's reach.

The moment she touched him, she knew it was Leandros, a sprawled and vacant mass. Just a few more backward, staggering steps and she hoped they were beyond the floodwaters, for a few minutes. Dragging him took the last burst of her energy, more necessity than strength.

She fell to his side, eyes searching his form, fingertips pressed to his neck. Beneath her touch bounced the faint but steady rhythm of his blood. An exhale of relief wrestled with her throat, raspy and wet, as the snakes leaned toward Leandros. Then escaped a laugh, short and sharp, strangled and wet, but he jostled as if in surprise.

His palm found her cheek quickly, impossibly so, and she leaned into the chilled curve of his hand. He strummed her skin as if she were an instrument, his own likely lost to the deluge.

I hope he can get another one, she thought without reason.

His lids fluttered under the raindrops, lips parting.

"You're here?" He spluttered the syllables, expression hazy.

The storm consumed the whisper of her name, yet she watched his mouth, and she knew what he'd said. She cradled him, brought her lips to his ear, and said, "I'm here. You're not alone. I have you, Leandros."

A breath tickled her ear. "I'm glad. You should call me Lee." And with the words, he slumped to the side in an apparent loss of consciousness.

***

Mixed with the inky smears of rainfall, a hulking darker mass

26

traversed the hills, lit by infrequent flashes of lights, pursued by the booms of thunder.

One of them had been in a river for several minutes and one had run through the downpour. Both were drenched, and nothing distinguished who had survived which situation. They dragged across the landscape, leaving impressions in the mud and the lowlands behind.

Medusa staggered over the plains, Lee's arm wrapped around her neck. She sagged from the weight, teeth grinding and back seizing. Lee was worse off. Blood leaked from a gash on his forehead, and his voice escaped in pained grunts. Some cuts were from his tussle with the dead man's brother, she guessed, others from his almost drowning.

He coordinated his legs eventually and managed a messy gait beside her. She ignored her own fatigue, suppressed the bile of fear and apprehension that formed in the pit of her stomach. To heft such a large man on a good day would have been a challenge. The effort while tired, goose-pimpled, and hungry was nearly impossible.

Her snakes nuzzled her, encouraging each step after step.

"Thank you," Lee said. It was his fifth round of thanks. She'd wager several gold coins there would be more.

"You mustn't say that. It's the least I can do after you..." She cut herself off and paused for both of their benefits.

He steadied his stance and touched his wrinkling forehead. "I don't know what I did. I can't—"

"Can't what?" She encircled his left wrist as the rain calmed somewhat. At least now she heard him without straining.

"I can't remember..." He stopped, freed his arm from her grasp, and spread his hands out in front of him. "Why can't I see?"

Medusa stood beside him, brows pinching at how he struggled to stay upright. She gripped his forearm, but he whipped it away. She recoiled, trying not to touch him more than necessary and yet very much wanting more.

His next question was a splinter lodged deep, a spear driven into the softest part of her. She feared it may never cease its echoes of pain, never stop hurting.

"Who are you?"

"You don't.... Know me?

He took a haphazard backward step. "No. Tell me now."

"I'm..." She considered giving a false name, but decided against it. Her response burned like swallowing an ember. "My name is

Medusa."

The answer didn't appear to register, for the lines on his face only deepened. He winced, holding his temples, and she guessed the discomfort was only going to increase. If he was searching for understanding, he didn't find it.

"What's happened?"

She moved her bottom lip back and forth between her teeth and said, "I think you hit your head in the river. I'm sure your memories will come back soon. But we have to get out of this storm."

"I'm so cold," he said, tone tight.

"I have a blanket at my home, and wood stashed out of the rain. We'll... Get through this, all right?" She hadn't convinced herself, and it seemed unlikely she would be any more successful with him.

"What happened to my eyes?" He waved a hand around in search of her, and she stepped closer so they could start moving again. He didn't resist her touch anymore.

Again, she paused, debating what and how much to say. "You told me a god took your sight. You didn't tell me why. I believe it was to punish you."

"A god?" His scoff sounded hollow. "What is so important about me that warrants retribution from the gods?"

"They don't always choose important people to hurt. I wasn't important, either. It doesn't stop them, who you are or what you did." Thunder crashed in the distance. "They take what they want and never acknowledge the suffering they cause."

She hissed the last words, and her companions wavered by her temples. She rarely spoke so freely about the gods, nor to people in general.

His head swiveled in her direction, but in the gloom, his vague expression stayed unreadable. She wasn't sure if she wanted to read it. There could be something frightening there.

"We'll talk more about anything you'd like to later," she said between huffs. "I'm tired and you're large. Let's get there, get warm, and then I'll answer what I can."

"And eat. I am starving."

He squeezed her arm, perhaps for balance, or reassurance, or desperation. She roiled with all the possibilities and the swarm of her snakes pricked her scalp. Hope shriveled up, horribly fast, as the serpents seemed to wail into the night.

That's when he heard them. His massive frame shook at the sound of sinuous bodies in motion.

"What was that?" he gasped.

Her body temperature seemed to drop further, and she shuddered as if ice replaced her bones. He moved back from her slowly, and her thoughts went vertiginous from the delayed understanding, leaving her unsure which direction was up or down. To remain standing took the entirety of her effort, sapping all that remained.

He'd entirely forgotten who she was. What she was.

He didn't know she was a monster.

Chapter 6

It was only a week ago that Medusa had found this place, deemed it sufficient, and claimed the pathetic house as hers. After days on the run, fleeing her last residence after the arrival of her almost murderers, it was a relief to find an isolated building at ocean's side. On its own, far-flung, like she was.

Now, her profound fatigue evaporated, replaced by a wild, surging glee. It was in sight, a soft white smear against the seascape beyond the cliff's edge, and they would make it, and everything would be fine. She held to the words as she clutched at him.

Lee had recovered some of his senses. He carried his own weight, mostly, and he no longer released prolonged groans with every step. But he retained his state of profound ignorance, questioning his name and all beyond. She sagged further from the dueling hurdles; how she'd ease the throb in his head, and remedy his amnesia.

There would be time for that, and the snakes slithered in a circle of reassurance. *When did you all decide Lee was acceptable?* To them, he had become someone to trust instead of to defend against or attack. They stroked her temples.

When did I decide the same thing?

"Where are we?" he asked.

"Close. The house isn't much, but it's better than the bottom of a river, or the ocean. So no complaining."

His brows shot up halfway to his hairline, but he said nothing in response, placing one bare foot in front of the other. Between the two of them, they possessed a single shoe. She wondered if later they would laugh about the circumstances, but she doubted it.

Rain fell in the midnight quiet, nestling them together. She tried to ignore how her heartbeat hadn't slowed in what seemed like hours, but whether it was from their current proximity or the looming removal of it, she refused to consider. Her shoulder rested in the crook of his armpit, his long arm finally warm across her back. Though he was taller, his torso rubbed hers like tapestries in a gale. Heat invaded her cheeks, and she was relieved no one witnessed her blush.

Medusa glanced sideways, noting the tendrils of his dark hair bisecting his pale face. Everything about him was askance after his near drowning. She curled her fingers inward, fighting the impulse to tuck his hair behind his ears. Instead, she swept her undulating halo farther away from him, and the small serpents followed the motion, favoring the left hemisphere of her scalp more than the other.

She hadn't explained their presence. He hadn't asked again.

*Once before he'd accepted me—man-killer, snake-woman—*she thought. *Can he do it a second time?*

The storm respected its uneasy peace with them as they passed through the crooked door. She coaxed Lee inside, her hands on his hips, to avoid him running into the decaying planks. He stiffened under her pressure, so subtly she might have imagined it.

"You're inside now," she said, barely audible. She gathered a candle and flint, and struck forth a flame. The sudden flare had no effect on his expression. She studied him as he dragged a palm across a wall.

"It doesn't feel like it."

For a moment, her nose pinched, fearing he was critiquing the house. But then she saw how his face pitched in response to the slight air invading the broken frame that had grown twice its original size over the years.

"The house needs work," she said, toeing the damp earthen floor. "But it's done me well, so far. I suppose even in the mud, I've found some security."

"Even in mud." He studied the space with his senses. "Will you do it? Fix it up?"

She didn't have an answer. Yes, she'd planned to. But after what had unfurled, this place wasn't safe.

"Here's a blanket," she said in distraction. It had sat underneath the most leak-resistant section of the roof on her thin pallet.

He reacted instinctively to collect the rough cloth before pausing. After a moment, he slanted closer, insistence lining his face.

"Thank you, but you should use it."

"Don't be silly. You almost drowned." She suppressed a shiver.

"Don't be stubborn," he said, lips quirking.

Medusa's nostrils flared, bristling most unlike her reptiles, who hissed their encouragement to accept his offer. Lee tilted away from the sound, his dark brows creasing.

"There are creatures here. Did they follow us?"

She bit her lip. "They won't hurt you. They're... with me."

"With you how?"

Curiosity softened his expression. *He believes me,* she thought, more hopeful than certain. *He trusts it is all right.*

In a rush of determination, Medusa decided to explain. To remove one of the biggest obstacles of her identity might have the added benefit of aiding his memory, she reasoned. But something acrid formed on her tongue nonetheless.

"I believed them a curse for too long," she said, watching the flickering light in the shadows, feeling his presence beside her. "But I soon realized how wrong I was. They are allies. They are part of me, perhaps even more than my family ever was."

He remained at a distance, tiny twitches moving through his muscles, the blanket daring her to seize it. The lack of reply made her skin tighten uncomfortably. Then he closed the gap between them, thrusting the blanket upward.

To her surprise, she snorted a laugh. "I'm not that tall."

Lee's lips pressed together as if he was suppressing a grin. "That much is obvious. I did just walk with you for quite a while."

Another round of an unfamiliar pluck drew out her next words. "Walk? I would call that stumbling."

A sincere laugh escaped him, his face turning to the ceiling. The tendons in his neck jumped, lids shuttered, and she gaped for several seconds as his amusement unspooled.

All the while, the blanket hung limp between them. She stuck out her hand to grab it, her own intractability thinning.

"We need to clean your face," she said. "You have cuts. They're not bleeding anymore—"

"I'm fine."

She narrowed her eyes briefly, settling on not pushing it.

Lee wiped his face with the remaining shreds of his shirt. A flash of his abdomen made her startle. She jerked her face away.

"Well, I will not fear them, your allies," he said, straightening his shirt once more. "I cannot fathom why, but I'm not afraid."

"I was afraid of you."

He considered this. "Then why would you save me from the river?"

She shuffled her feet, mourning her lost shoe to the mud, and dropped the last flimsy strip of leather by the door.

"I was wrong."

"How do you know me? And I you?"

A loud gust shot through the crevices and broken panes. They trembled in response.

She swung the fabric over her shoulder and touched his arm, guiding him to the driest corner. Touch itself seemed a transgression. He didn't remember who she was, was ignorant of the danger she posed. A deep part of her splintered as he flinched in her grip. *So recently he defended me, sacrificed himself for me.*

"We met today. You…" Suddenly light-headed, she guided him to sit. "You said you'd come looking for me."

"Why?"

"You believed we had something in common."

When she lowered the worn, scratchy fabric to his shoulders, he didn't resist. He barely noticed, seemingly too committed to listening.

Her voice was unsteady, betraying her disorderly emotions. From her shelves she gathered some bits to eat while he stayed silent in the corner. She poured a stash of berries onto a battered metal plate, piled on a few dried fish, and grabbed her jug of fresh water. The noises, louder than the now dull patter of rain, swept over his impassive frame.

"I wish I could remember," he said.

It escaped as a whisper, likely inaudible if she hadn't drawn nearer. Her bare feet cooled on the compacted mud floor.

"As do I." She set the jug by his foot. "Water to drink."

He nodded once, but didn't move to retrieve it.

Impatiently, she took his hand, rolled out his fingers, and put the plate on his upturned palm.

"Food. Berries, fish. I'm sorry there's nothing better."

He hovered over the plate, sniffing. "Hmm. I can tell you it's superior to than anything I've had in quite a few years."

Medusa contorted her fingers at her lower back, the snakes churning from her scalp to their tongues.

"Thank you," he said, before taking a bite.

She wouldn't have let herself stare if he were a sighted person, but she deemed the impolite behavior innocent in tone. His lips worked the food slowly, his teeth gradually emulsifying the various components of his lackluster meal. Another burning shard raced through her heart as he savored the flecks of fish, the crush of berries.

"You can't possibly understand how kind you are," he said at last, scraping the plate for crumbs.

"This isn't that kind," she countered. "Feeding someone in need? That doesn't make me worthy of praise."

"Hmm."

She averted her gaze as he licked his fingertips. All at once, the chilled wind infiltrating the structure was insufficient. She needed the frigid slap of seawater to jolt her from this abrupt and encompassing physical heat.

With the empty plate, he rose to his feet, wedged the blanket into his elbows, and approached. She blinked as he walked directly to her shelves of food and prepared another plate.

"I'm sorry I didn't share. It's very rude," he said. "Will you eat? You must be hungry, too."

Lee completed his task and settled into the corner again, one hand holding her meal aloft, the other opening a wing of the blanket.

The snakes bounced, demonstrating her own desperate need for food and warmth.

"Please?"

The prompt swept all other thoughts away, all hesitation.

"If you insist." She let the snake's enthusiasm set their pace. *So impatient,* she inwardly scolded her companions, but gratitude accompanied her.

Medusa fit into the space beside him under the arch of his blanketed embrace. Already they had been close, held one another as they hurried to shelter. Of course, that had occurred in the chaos of before, spurred by fear and anxiety.

That had changed. Here it was stillness, quiet, the most casual she expected they could ever be.

If only he remembered.

She chewed the food, grateful for anything to defeat her gnawing hunger. He was easy to please, for the food was unflavored, the fish was cold, and the berries under-ripe. But it filled her belly steadily, and she stifled a yawn as she finished.

Neither spoke for several minutes. They breathed like branches entwined, not identical, but similar enough to complement.

"And what of you?" Lee's question jolted her. "Have you experienced generosity?"

"What do you mean?" She leaned back to see more of his face.

"You said what you gave me isn't worth praising. That must mean you also recognize what is worthy."

She fiddled with the edge of her empty plate. "No, few people are kind. I suppose I don't know what is generous, other than you saving my life."

"I saved your life?"

Another stab of mourning something lost coursed through her and she forcefully ignored it. "You protected me from someone attacking. And I didn't get to thank you."

"I must... care about you." This was threateningly similar to a statement rather than a question. "I think I can trust that, at least."

She jerked her gaze forward to focus on a misaligned layer of stones near the ceiling. "I cannot say. But you went into that river because of me. The least I could do was help you out of it."

"I understand."

The ensuing break in conversation prickled, yet there was no way to gauge who hurt more, or even why. Her snakes drooped to her shoulders, too weary to stay upright.

Her stomach bunched in on itself. The chill clung tighter, the fire of embarrassment having faded minutes prior. Without preamble, her wet clothes became a discomfort that demanded remedying.

He shifted as if he too recognized this issue, and adjusted his shirt. His shoulder rubbed hers, signaling his gradual slide to a hunch on the floor. She noted how his thumb tapped his raised knee.

To guess he was nervous caught her as absurd. *I hardly know enough about people to say for sure,* she thought.

The rain on the roof softened further but the landscape outside kept its shadowy gauze. It was merely the two of them, snakes beginning to slumber.

He released a low kind of hum akin to contentment.

Her heart hammered hard enough to pulse her fingertips. She was getting hot once more, her shivers submitted to the heat between them, their layers of wet clothes seemingly disappeared. The violent swinging from one state of being to another left her dizzy.

"I'm sorry it's dirty," she said out of necessity.

"No more apologies, please." He wiggled his elbow against hers as if in comfort. "You saved me, sheltered me. I'm no longer cold or hungry. I can ask for nothing else."

He shifted in her direction and his exhale sent goosebumps down her arm.

"Asking for answers makes sense," she said. "But I have few to provide."

Lee unnecessarily tucked the blanket around her, igniting feverish flickers as he did so.

"Perhaps starting with what you know is the best. If you're comfortable with that."

Fatigue laced his voice.

"Or we sleep first," she said.

He chuckled, then tilted toward her. She rested her head atop his, smelling the earth, stones, and their bodies. The last thing she knew was the draping of her snakes upon Lee, asleep beside her.

Chapter 7

The sound of jostling clay jars woke her.

She squinted and raised an arm over her face, the sun slanting through the patchy thatch of the roof.

Medusa jerked upright. She lay on the pallet, fully clothed, but curled into herself toward the wall. The blanket stretched over her, and half of the pallet was empty.

"I'm sorry," Leandros said over his shoulder. He fumbled about the cupboards, chin to his chest as he searched. "I was hoping to find an alternate option for breakfast."

"We ate everything last night," she said, swept up in a battle of emotions.

Last night.

Driven by exhaustion, distress, near madness, she had rested beside a stranger. Her sinuous crown stretched contentedly in the yellow-infused light, accepting how damp and stuffy the house was. They seemed utterly unperturbed by her brazen behavior.

She ducked her head, horrified by the new pattern of color rising in her cheeks. The previous hours had swept by so quickly, and most of the morning, by the looks of it. With a start, she realized there was no nightmare, no vision of the man intending to kill her. An additional surprise that was difficult to comprehend—a restful night's sleep.

She hoped he slept well, too, but couldn't form those particular words.

"We can forage for more. Then perhaps... we wash our clothes."

"You don't fear the river after the flood?" He retrieved the jug of water and handed it to her.

"I know there is a smaller stream that leads into the river, cuts through the eastern section of the forest. That should be enough for us to wade in."

"I welcome shallow. I'd rather not introduce any more opportunities to drown." He paused, arms hanging awkwardly at his sides. "Though I don't regret jumping into that river. Not if it was to…"

"Stop a man from attacking me." She grasped jug's neck, growing heavy from the memory.

"Why *was* he attacking?" Lee asked, pressing nearer.

Being direct and honest was the best approach, she concluded. "I disposed of his brother."

"Oh."

She darted a look at him, willing there to be no vitriol or judgement in response to her statement. Lee's expression was impassive, distant, and he rocked into a seated position.

"The brother wanted to hurt me," she said in a rush.

"Why is that what people want to do?"

Because of what I am, she thought.

A more suitable answer refused to arrive. Despite her restorative sleep, her mind muddied of its own accord. She did warn that man who materialized what seemed like years ago, but without repeated effort. Instead, she'd let him die. *Killed him,* she silently corrected.

And that only led to further death.

Good riddance, a part of her countered. *But what is the cost,* an opposing part said.

"These men believe life would be better if I'd never existed," she said following a long silence. Her throat itched with the confession. She swung the jug up for multiple gulps.

"That can't be true."

The snakes wove into themselves as she slid off the pallet onto her knees. If he could see her, she fretted it would look like pleading. She swept away the concern.

"I won't defend my actions," she said, but her tone undercut the message.

"I shouldn't ask you to. There are things I've done that I can't recall." He shrugged. "Probably worse things."

She imagined watching the stone man plummet to the craggy shore below, the spike of thrill knowing he couldn't harm her anymore.

"I'm not sure about that."

The autumnal brown of his eyes dimmed, his brows twitching. A few inches separated them, the gap filled with a bright midday glimmer. She stood in a flurry, and Lee startled.

"I have to get food," she said over her grumbling stomach. "You stay here. It won't be long."

He swept upright, both hands suspended. "If I may, I will come with you. Please."

You'll slow me down, she thought. A cruel assumption. "You don't know the way."

"Once I did."

"How can you know that? Do you remember something?"

He paused, fiddling with the ragged edge of his previously white shirt. "No, it's more of a feeling. Should we trust it?"

"Like you trust yourself that I am safe?" The question struck both of them. She glanced at the floor, and said, "Fine, yes, you can come." It wasn't worth debating. They could sit wherever she found an edible morsel and eat right away. She almost smiled at the notion. Stars, she was hungry.

He picked up her scavenging bag from its place on a shelf, and offered it to her. She draped it over her shoulder in its usual orientation, her smile eking out, as if withdrawn by his movement, just at the corners of her mouth.

"You already feel your way around my house."

"It's rather easy. There's not much here," he said, tone jocular.

It was his turn to release a grin, but he directed it away from her.

The exchange was a reminder of his comment the night before, when she initially thought he was mocking her. But this was different, akin to her recent tease.

There was an unnamed cadence brewing, reminiscent of intimacy.

I shouldn't overthink, she chided.

Medusa adjusted her bag, took his wrist, and ushered him outside. This time, there was no flinch. He only followed in her wake, accepting where she led him.

***

The forest enveloped them in saturated depths. Puddles of water seeped forth, birds fluttered rain from their wings, and branches sprinkled them anew with each rush of wind.

Medusa released him, perturbed by the contagious quality of his inexplicable warmth. Inexplicable, by every parameter she identified.

Nothing made sense.

An orange hue caught her attention, and she lurched toward a clump of mushrooms sprouting between tree trunks, hoping he wouldn't notice her sudden shift. But her shoulders fell as she recognized this variety as poisonous.

"Inedible," she said.

They continued their walk, Lee trailing behind, seemingly tracking the sounds she made. She walked slower than usual, not wanting him to feel abandoned. Just as he suggested, he navigated the forest with ease, tripping rarely over an upturned root or colliding with a twisted branch.

"How are you doing that?" she asked, startling particles floating in a shaft of light. Her snakes playfully nipped at the mix of pollen, dust, and whatever else flurried around them.

"Doing what?"

"Navigating the forest." She swerved around a too-friendly bee. "It's almost as if you can see everything."

What terrible phrasing, she thought with horror.

"You mean I should stumble more?" The jest tilted his words upward. He raised his shoulders, a futile gesture, and dropped them.

"Of course," she said, voice lowering. "You don't remember."

"There's a smell," he said, weight added to the words. "It's familiar. Perhaps I explored this forest... Before this." He gestured at his face.

She floundered for a response and came up short. Gaze flicking where they'd paused, she said, "I found some blossoms nearby. They have a lemony flavor."

"And how does lemon taste?" He came to a stop, turning his head in her direction and smacking his temple against a jagged twig. "Curses!" he yelped, and knelt on the ground.

She was beside him in a moment. "Lee," Medusa said, crouching beside his doubled over body. He pressed against the wound, but tiny red drops leaked between his fingers. "You're bleeding again. You just keep adding more scratches to your face. Let me see."

The command worked instantly. He dropped his arms, wincing against the slink of blood into his left eye. It arched over his eyebrow with jagged edges. Her companions hissed to lap at the crimson drip. Mortified by their lack of propriety, Medusa shook them, and tore a handful of velvety leaves from a low, squat plant, then pressed the soft fibrous patch to the cut.

"This will help stop the flow."

He released a sharp breath. "I guess I was wrong about knowing my way."

His response sent a wisp of breath down her wrist. She swallowed, so hard she feared he heard it, and changed her position on the ground. Rainfall soaked the knees of her skirt, staining the already dulled fabric. She guessed there was nothing attractive about her current bedraggled state, and it was off-putting to even consider her appearance.

It was disquieting to admit that kind of worry was more foreign than anything else that was transpiring.

She appraised Lee as he held himself, face down-turned, cheeks growing ruddy.

"It's all right. I should have helped," she said.

The leaves, partially saturated, collected no further blood. He fumbled in search of the makeshift bandage and she opened her hand to let him touch the mess.

"What a wonder."

"Nature has much to offer."

"I didn't mean that."

He curled his fingers around the leaves. She couldn't tell if he meant to touch her or not, but the result was a fresh wave of ripples down her form.

His tone held whimsy again. "I'll be fine, I'm sure."

Medusa surged to stand, dropping the leaves, and searching their surroundings. She forced a chuckle through her dry mouth and worried he'd interpret it as a choke.

"Should I take your hand?" she heard herself ask as if at a great distance.

Please say yes.

A muscle tensed on his jaw and he fiddled with a nearby sapling before quickly saying, "Don't worry, I'll keep up."

She nodded, though he couldn't observe it, and wiped her hands on her skirt. "I haven't found much for breakfast, let alone a midday meal. Let's keep looking."

Her legs pumped, a frenzied pulse in every limb. Sunshine steamed the forest, thickening the air and her breathing. She'd missed it after days of rain, though this temperature conjured a drowsiness, but the rumble in her belly kept her moving. Focus falling to a particularly nutritious reed and a clump of clover nearby, she grinned and knelt down to harvest. She plucked a mouthful of the plant to chew as she worked the reeds out. They would be better if soaked and hammered into mush and dried to make cakes, but it was something. With one pull, she dispatched the clover and shoved it into her bag.

She looked behind her, expecting Lee to arrive, yet saw no one on the path. Instant panic erupted, coursing from her toes into the very tips of her snakes. Their distress tightened her scalp.

"Lee?" Her yell echoed between the trunks. "Leandros?"

Birdsong was the only reply. Then—

"Over here," he called. "In the creek."

She froze, and hear it, a shallow babble over rocks. It sounded louder than the trickle she'd come across during her first exploration of the forest.

I wonder if it's deep enough to wash off, she thought. Mud flaked from her in dry patches, and her clothes resembled kindling to start a fire. The chance to clean grew more enticing than breakfast. Nonetheless, she chewed another mouthful of clover, saving the rest for Lee.

"Medusa?" he said, voice jostled by the swish of branches.

"Coming." She left the path, sculpted narrowly from deer hooves, and followed his voice.

I should have packed soap.

He sat on a rocky bank, feet submerged in the creek. It had a brownish tint after the heavy rain, having eaten away at the land in the floodwater's haste. His torn sleeves were rolled to the elbows, tawny skin on display. A gap in the canopy settled him in a blanket of sun. He reclined, perfectly at ease, more comfortable than she'd seen him.

"A good find," she said, unsure what exactly she meant by the words.

"Indeed." He smiled, lids closed a few seconds more. Finally, he turned toward her. "Will you join me?"

Her heart clenched like vines gripping a trunk.

Instead of forcing herself to speak, she walked closer, trying to ignore how her living halo coursed with anticipation. Of what, she wasn't ready to address.

Medusa arrived beside him, slightly upstream, and bent her legs. She submerged her hands, catching some between her palms, and splashed her face, relishing the coolness. Her next urge was to scrub every inch of her body, but she sat beside Lee. He stretched his legs farther into the depths.

"I… I remember this place. It rarely flows like this."

She gave him a sidelong glance. Her snakes spread out in the light, expanding like prongs. In the subsequent quiet, she wiggled her ankles into the flowing water. Her feet didn't ache, being used to lots of bare walking, but her back did.

A loud crack stirred up the revery, and Medusa jolted. Her gaze followed squirrels tussling, two furred forms that scurried out of sight.

Lee didn't react, seemingly lost to a different time.

"I have memories… The aroma of these woods, the arrangement of these rocks," he said, almost wistful. "But I still can't conjure anything about you."

She swallowed, plunged an arm into the water, and snatched a rock. It was rough, unremarkable, streaked by gray-green lines. Plain and bumpy and cracked. She'd take that over being a cursed creature.

A sensation settled over her, like lightning trapped in a lofty cloud.

"Trust me, it's a gift to forget who I am."

He drew nearer, an increasingly noticeable muscle jumping under his eye. "Why?"

It was a fluke, you accepting what I am.

With a swift toss, she let the rock go. It splashed off the other bank, disappearing into the flow.

"Maybe if you told me something," he urged, "it would help my memories return."

The idea was logical, but she resisted the suggestion for several more seconds. She slipped into the water until it lapped at her shins, swirling the short hair growing there.

Either she risked telling him the truth, and his initial interest in knowing her dissolved. Or she lied. She dared not stay with him, that was clear. She didn't think she could bear his inevitable expression of disgust, fear.

Rejection.

But she had come too far in accepting the sharpness of her reality. There would be no falsehoods with Lee.

She spoke into the stillness.

"You'd heard stories about me in the village where you lived. From others across the countryside. That's my guess. You understood what I can do, what made me different. I can kill a man with only a glance." She spoke haltingly, but didn't stop. "They perceive me and promptly become stone. I have spent the last two years of my life running from my horrors, only to create more wherever I go."

His body remained stiff, unbreathing, un-reacting. When he shifted himself toward her, she tensed, ready to run. She'd left almost everything behind already. Leandros would be just another bit of sea glass upon the beach of her life. If that was necessary, she would do it.

But she never would have expected him to lay his hand on hers.

Chapter 8

Time stretched between them, languid as honey, and similarly sweet.

She allowed his pressure to soak in, to saturate her skin, blood, bones. Though his pupils didn't focus on her, she sensed the layer of his awareness tangibly. To be perceived, discerned, *realized* made her head swirl.

"I cannot understand much," Lee said, running a fingertip over her knuckles. "All I have is the truth of before. If I knew this about your identity, I accept it now."

Medusa's snake carried themselves aloft, raucous as her own mind. As Lee extended a finger, the bravest of them, which sprouted from near her temple, wiggled closer. She bit her tongue until blood erupted, an insufficient distraction from his approach.

Her companions had never willingly allowed a person's caress. A dark, buried part of her feared they would strike, to defend her and the possibility of astounding emotional pain.

"Are you sure...?" But her question died before completion.

The snake's tongue tickled Lee's finger, and his lips parted.

"So your hair is... alive?"

She nodded, despite his inability to see the gesture. As if reassured, his hand wove deeper into the living strands, creating a pattern of light brown skin and green hued scales. The action, rippling from the top of her spine to her hairline, was so sublime she questioned if she was awake.

"They're snakes," he said, tone both unbelieving and awed. "They're connected to you."

"They weren't at first." Her breath shook. "I hated them." Despite the years, this confession still hurt to acknowledge, but the snakes ignored the prick of the truth, undulating around Lee's presence, inviting him deeper.

"It was a change," he said, nodding slowly. "I hated losing my sight."

Medusa drifted into the touch, his thumb grazing her ear.

He withdrew in a flash, cheeks flushing a sunburnt color. "I'm sorry. How terribly rude—"

"It's all right," she said, but the claim rang false. Her entire form trembled from his withdrawal.

"I knew you were powerful. I hope I..." His jaw muscle jumped, and he positioned himself toward the opposite bank. A bead of sweat crept down his forehead, one that mimicked the drips down her spine. It was late morning, and the heat was worsening.

So too her hunger.

"What?" she said, rummaging in her bag for the clover and reeds. With effort, her voice stayed neutral, relaxed, but her thoughts screamed to know what he intended to say.

He pulled at a loose thread on his sleeve. "Before. I'm afraid I coveted your power."

She had dreaded him saying something much worse. "No, not at all." She considered her next words. "You seemed more... fascinated. Drawn to it... as if you believed it was a bond that required strengthening."

Her throat dried as the statement settled. The claim was brazen, yet he did not scoff, he smiled.

"It is the same now."

Neither spoke for a while. Birdsong seemed to swell, the grass softened, and their patch of shade deepened. She glanced at him, pushing her lips into a line. Beyond all rationality, she wished to fold herself into him, claim him, as she had when dragging him from the flood.

The gap separating them felt like it shrank. She gathered his hand and deposited the food—knowing it wasn't enough—and purposefully looked anywhere else but at him.

Minutes followed the creek elsewhere, lulling her into a state of grateful reprieve. The food didn't last long, as he poured the items into his mouth and chewed as he draped his elbows on his upraised knees. She tried not to stare, forcing herself to nibble on a reed stalk.

"I have an idea," Lee said.

She peered at him. "What?"

He gave her a small, impish smile, stood, and entered the creek.

Despite being fully clothed, he waded into the silted water until he was submerged to his hips. Though not wide, the creek was deep after the storm.

She watched, astonished, as he splashed himself. Water trickled lower, taking a long, steady journey down his body, making his skin gleam. The black strands of his hair stuck together like limp serpents. A blush erupted from her collar bones at the vision.

"I couldn't resist. I probably stink something awful," he said, the smile widening.

And I am just as bad. Her revealed flesh prickled from the afternoon heat as the creek gurgled its invitation. His courage was contagious. *Contagious things are rarely good,* she warned out of habit.

But she had already caught whatever it was.

She grasped her skirt and slipped in after him.

***

Medusa trembled as the wavelets swept around her. She settled her footing on the rocky bottom and stretched out both arms for balance. The temperature was initially frigid, but as she pushed forward, her muscles relaxing.

Lee stepped out of the deeper middle, perhaps sensing she was close. He kept his eyes averted. Even with his lack of sight, he apparently offered her privacy.

"How does it feel?"

She steadied herself in the swift current and enjoyed a full breath. "Nice. It was a good idea."

His arms swirled on the bubbling surface, cresting the wavelets that churned with abandon. Briefly, he looked ready to speak, but he opted for a rapid dunk instead.

Laughter burst out of her before his head resurfaced a few feet downstream.

"I didn't expect you wanting to get wet for a while."

Lee snorted. "Me either." He returned to their now comfortable proximity, splashing with each step. A few flecks landed on her collarbone, and she considered mimicking his plunge. As she debated scrubbing her hair, he spoke again.

"Do you mind if I...?" He gestured vaguely at his torso.

Medusa said, "No," before she discerned what he meant.

The flash of partial nudity caught her off guard. She stumbled into the depths, averting her focus from his newly revealed chest. This was a much more thorough display than the previous night. He tossed the ripped shirt to the bank and dove under again.

As he disappeared, his dark hair a seaweed mass, she didn't take her eyes off him. He reappeared a few seconds later, and she stared at the expanse of his bare skin. She understood how large he was, having bolstered his weight already. But the sight of him invited a heavy blush that invaded with haste. She pivoted, attention landing on a surprising bunch of soapwort, and hurried to pluck out the plant, splashing loudly as she went.

"What it is?" he said, riffling his wet hair.

She tugged it out with satisfaction, and glanced at him. "A plant we can use for soap."

"What luck." His smile made the sentence round and buoyant.

Tearing her gaze from his expression, she halved the stalks, making a knotted bunch for each of them, then rubbed the wads into thick suds.

"Here," she said, administering the lather on his shoulders.

He became still as earth under her fingertips, and she quickly went rigid.

"Sorry," she rushed to say, flailing in embarrassment and jerking the mixture up before losing it to the water. Horror clung to her, the crown of snakes writhing as Medusa stepped back.

"I'm sorry. I wasn't thinking—"

"All is fine, and you can stay, if you're comfortable. You'll do a better job than I could." His grip found her wrist, fingers overlapping where her tendons were. She trembled, as did he, but neither broke the point of contact.

"You want me to...?"

He worked his mouth, lips caught between his teeth for a moment. "If it doesn't bother you, I would be exceedingly grateful."

She hesitated, and his entire upper half reddened.

"It's too forward. I'm sorry to ask." The words came with a tremor. "And it would jeopardize..." He broke off.

"What?"

"If... someone saw us—"

"Ah." She regretted the tumult of confusing, red emotions. "Well, if it's a man, he'll die on the spot." *If it's a woman,* she thought, *she'd judge me worse for my snakes than bathing with a stranger.*

But *stranger* didn't seem an accurate term to describe Leandros anymore.

Medusa brushed the snakes from her face, their tickling excitement too much.

"It's a fair request," she said, seizing the opportunity despite heat swirling in her belly. "We can reach places on the other we can't on ourselves."

What silly reasoning.

Lines formed on the bridge of his nose, demonstrating his reticence. "If you're sure. I would hate to make you uncomfortable—"

"It's fine," she said firmly. "I don't mind. My sisters always reminded me to be helpful."

His full lips bunched, hesitating once more, before he nodded and rotated the other direction.

The sun delighted in illuminating him, all warm hues and soft glimmers. Lee's back was more pale than his forearms, and flecked with freckles. To her bewilderment, she itched to trace them. She held the soapwort harder, making suds and spreading the lather. There were bruises and scrapes from his floodwater trip and she made a note to check them later for infection. Multiple remedies that might speed up healing sprang to mind. *It would be another excuse to touch him too,* she realized. Her snakes wove a bramble on her scalp, perhaps thrilled or anxious at the prospect.

"You're hurt," she said too quietly.

"It's nothing."

He stayed frozen as she spread the soap on the middle of his back. Any lower would be obscene and the mere thought sent sparks through her, fierce as a blade forged by fire. An opposing visual joined this, that the water scoured away any traces of dirt. It was doing the same for her, she guessed.

But her torn shirt was discolored by dried mud and untouched by water save for the bottom edge. She dismissed the worry, and said, "I can wash your neck, too."

He lowered himself to give her access, which made them closer to the same height, and she worried his knees would start hurting soon.

Under her palm, the mud flaked off the plains of his form. She had to move onto her toes to swipe the leftover dirt from his hairline. She refocused on his immediacy, tracing the bumps of his spine with her fingers. They reminded her of the snakes, a steady undulation of existence. The sensation demanded more, and before she noticed, her movements had grown feather soft and insistent.

"You might be forgetting the soap," he said, barely a whisper.

"Forgive me." Her voiced was a rasp. To cover her mounting shame, she pressed the soapwort into his palm and retrieved his dirty shirt to situate it in the gentle eddies of the rocks. Distantly, she recognized the sound of branches crunching, most likely a deer. She swallowed the snap of worry.

"It's silly to clean ourselves if our clothes remain filthy," she said as she worked.

He blinked, as if understanding was a bright flare of light that even he could sense.

"Of course," he said, pressing the soap mass to his front.

The motions were hurried, transfixing. She regretted not offering to do that part, too.

His next words poured out of him. "It's kind of you to wash my clothes. I'll give you space if you want to take yours off. I'll sit by a tree, if that helps. I'll even turn the other way, but you don't have to clean your clothes. Not that you smell—"

She laughed and found an answer quicker than expected. "I can't say they're anything but filthy. I'm not offended."

Before she could talk herself out of the sequence of events, she pulled her shirt off. The snakes jostled, both from the movement and apprehension. Next she tugged off her pants, leaving only her undergarments.

"You can toss me your pants," she said, sounding far more confident than she felt. "They need soap."

"Do they?" His voice grew muffled over the creek. "You're right, I'm sure…"

After a brief struggle, he removed the torn pants. Whatever he wore beneath remained shrouded in the water. Medusa searched for another clump of soapwort, her body shaking.

She scampered to uproot more of the plant and rubbed it upon the clothes until the fibers loosened. They embraced the quiet as she situated their clothing. It wouldn't be long for them to get clean, she reasoned, but drying would add time.

How quickly she'd forgotten the need to leave this place.

With a glance toward Leandros, she returned to the water, leaving a gap between them. She crouched, sunk under the surface, letting the current dance through her snakes. When she rose for air, Lee's palm stretched to her.

"The soap... It's almost all gone."

"Oh, of course." She noted how she shook, but not because of a threat of violence. It was want, vivid as sunrise. For the first time in years, she craved the simplicity of physical contact.

Sensing her hesitation, he said, "If you aren't comfortable—"

She reached for him. "I am. It might not make any sense, but I'm comfortable."

He released an exhale, relief softening his nervous expression. She turned, offering him her back, and covered her breasts, fists under her chin. All she knew was his gentle movements, leaving blossoms of thrill along her veins. His attention was delicate, diligent, like coaxing a song from an instrument. Her insides sung in response, her arms loosening, heart rate speeding. Some of his breath caught on her neck and the miniature hairs stood on end. She tensed without meaning to.

He paused, hovering nearby and yet too far away. "Should I stop?"

"No," she said. "It's... Lovely."

The word failed to convey anything at all. This wasn't like a star bisecting the sky, nor was it a spread of colorful flowers across a hill. This was being adored, this washing, this intimacy of cleaning one another.

He resumed, releasing handfuls of water to chase the bubbles away. A sting of tears accompanied the rinse. Just days prior, she expected to never invite someone, let alone a man, to lay hands on her ever again.

Yet here she was, glistening in the afternoon glow, wishing Lee would never stop.

Chapter 9

"What a helpful little plant."

Leandros held the last of the soapwort, thumbing the textured foliage. His head tilted upward, lips slightly parted, relishing the minutiae of the stem and leaves. He wore his pants and shirt, which were less stained, but a good soap washing wouldn't fix the rips. Medusa glimpsed a bit of his skin peeking through the tattered hem and suppressed a riotous surge from overwhelming all other senses. She adjusted her own clothes, then plucked a small strand of grass, murmuring in delayed agreement. The two of them settled in the sunshine to let their clothes dry while her snakes basked as well, still enough to be forgotten.

"Soapwort has been reliably helpful wherever I've gone." She nodded, if only for her own benefit. "Cleaned all the wounds I've gotten."

"I'm sorry," he said.

She eyed him, willing him to say more.

"That you've had to run for so long," he added.

Her lids fluttered shut, pushing against the rush of images. Watching Poseidon through the blur of tears leave the temple as she huddled in his wake. The smear of her childhood home disappearing amongst the waves as she hurried away. The patchwork of faces chasing her from hovel to hovel.

I may never be safe again. The stone of knowledge sunk down her throat, at once painful and familiar.

But there was no chance to dwell.

A crash shook the trees, followed by an onrushing slice of a sword. She rolled instinctively, knocking her head on the sharp rocks, but missing the blade that flashed in the light. The weapon quickly withdrew.

"You have escaped for some a few years now, it's true," a vitriol-soaked voice said.

She scrambled upright as Lee fumbled to stand.

"Who are you?" she said through snarling teeth. The forest suddenly seemed darker, more sinister. Powerlessness sprung forth, and rage that she had let herself relax.

She couldn't identify the speaker, but she knew it was a man. A man who knew enough to avert his gaze. She retreated a step, the snakes a writhing mass. Flashes of her reoccurring nightmare struck, stealing the breath from her lungs.

It's him. He's found me. Her snakes spat at the attacker, and a sour flavor coated her tongue. She seemed physically incapable of saying his name aloud.

"I know you, Medusa. I am your reckoning." The man's claim roiled more fiercely than the creek. "Tasked with bringing you to justice for all you have murdered."

Yes, I know you are, she thought, limbs stiffening. She distantly cursed her lack of reaction, that when it counted most, she failed to flee. Her body turned to stone in its own way, distilled into a pure and useless fear.

She had fought for survival for years, pulling herself up from the floor of Athena's temple after Poseidon's violation, to the next moment, and the next. There was always another urgency to fight on.

Now, fatigue dragged her downward, tugged to the earth, to the demise of this hero of her nightmares represented.

This will be the last.

Part of her invited this reckoning, couldn't fight it for a single additional moment. She shut out the world, relinquishing herself to what seemed inevitable.

"You will not hurt her," Lee said, making her jump.

She'd forgotten he was there, shaking beside her, chest heaving uncharacteristically.

He wedged himself in front of her, as if sensing the physical distress, her immobility. He circled his arms behind and around her, an act of defense. She trembled and clung to him, grateful at least to seize his immediacy.

Despite Lee's natural defense against her uncontrollable power, he still wasn't safe in her presence.

No one will ever be.

"Perseus," she said at last. The name lashed the air. "Don't kill Lee. Let him go."

A large reflective shape glinted, like a shield, between the trees as he moved closer. *Such a simple trick,* she mused darkly. The man would protect himself and use her own gaze against her.

As if falling into place, her wrath resurfaced, and with it, her determination.

No. I will not die by your hands.

"You have my word I will not kill the man," Perseus said. "Keep your face down or else I plunge my blade through his throat. That's the only warning I offer."

She placed a hand on her chest, giving him a gesture of confirmation, an attempt to communicate to Perseus without alerting Lee to where she stood.

"Medusa, no," Lee began, voice frayed as an old rope. He attempted to catch her, but she slipped from his grasp.

Lead him away from Lee, she outlined in her mind. *Protect him once more.*

"Don't do this," Lee said, tone pleading. He leaned an ear in her direction. She assumed he was listening, intending to decipher any disturbance. She stepped softer than before, touching down her toes first and bending onto her heels last, putting her many years of skills to use once more.

To keep her promise to the attacker, she stared at the ground, easing herself under the shadowed canopy.

"Closer," Perseus said. "You shall lay on the ground, cast in the mud, where you belong."

The corner of her mouth pinched as she neared the man's hiding place. He'd struck once already and missed. Perhaps she could out-maneuver him a second time.

She pressed her nails into her palms, deciding on her final words to Lee.

"Even in the mud we find safety," she said over her shoulder and louder than necessary.

Lee's head whipped in her direction, forehead creasing.

Please grasp my meaning, she thought toward him.

Perseus made a noise of impatience. Still, she lowered herself slowly, poised and patient, for the man to draw nearer. He stepped within range, shield a golden reflective orb separating them. Closer still.

Once she was almost prostrate, she looked under her armpit and kicked the attacker from below.

With a shriek, the man fell forward

Then she started running.

***

Branches whipped past in a flurry of stings and scratches, while her living halo seethed in displeasure. Her clothes, still wet, snagged and tore further. Though her feet were callused, she felt the sharpness of broken twigs with every hurried step.

Perseus followed, relentless as a dog. He didn't thrash or utter a sound, and she guessed he was skilled in navigating such dense woods. She tried to imagine his face from her nightmares and saw merely the icy shards of his irises. This man, a hero lauded by the people of his realm, was exceptionally capable, clever, and enterprising, more than any who pursued her previously. Even if she outran him, a task that was proving quite challenging, he wouldn't ever stop.

Medusa's breath came in great gasps after a few minutes. She led him deeper into the forest, in the opposite direction of the coast, keeping the flowing stream to her right. At some point, she slowed with the realization that she was possibly veering too close to the town Leandros had left. She pivoted and nearly crashed into a massive tree. With a pause that could allow him to catch up, she glanced upward, she noted its thick branches, and climbed before she questioned the change of plan.

I'll make sure he doesn't follow us anymore, she swore as she ascended the branches. The smooth limbs were a suitable ladder, and she found a speedy rhythm with ease. Below, she spotted Perseus arriving at the trunk, the flash of his silver shield bouncing. She paused, waiting for his next move.

"That is an intriguing choice, Gorgon," Perseus said, panting.

The use of her family name made her blood boil.

"I can wait for you here. Or perhaps I will return to your love? His cries from pain might bring you down from your lofty perch." Perseus lowered the shield, keeping his attention on the trunk. "Or maybe I will come after you alone. That's what you are. Alone. And there's no reason to delay the inevitable."

"I heard you," she said, trying to steady her voice. "Long before you attacked. I dismissed it, assuming it was nothing. Why did you wait?"

"Truthfully?" Perseus crouched and peered at the dirt. "I had to be sure it was you."

She scoffed. "You couldn't tell by the snakes?"

He paused, as if deliberating his reply. "I had to comprehend why that man wasn't dead."

"He's blind," she snapped.

"I understood that eventually. What a pity he doesn't understand who—what—you are."

"He does. I explained." Her knuckles were white, wrapped around a limb, ignoring how her head buzzed. "I told him everything."

"Well, then I cannot claim to understand him either. You cast a spell on him and I will free him of it." Perseus studied his shining blade, which showed no signs of blood.

"I didn't want to kill all those men."

Her words rasped. Perseus sneered.

"You admit it, all the unnecessary, horrific deaths. And how many have you killed? You should confess before I take your life."

"You won't take anything."

"Oh? You appear to be trapped in a tree. There are no stories about your ability to fly or become an animal. There is no escape." Perseus paused, running a thumb over the edge of his sword. "Tell me how many you've killed."

I've never kept track, she thought. The vice of her past clinched tighter until even breath became a struggle. Regret, horror, rage, and shame splintered her mind, disparate pieces separating, pulling apart. Her eyes slammed shut, causing bright sparks to form in the ensuing darkness. She bit her tongue until the discomfort rooted her in the present moment. The snakes churned, lending a cacophony to the otherwise quiet, before she set her gaze below.

Her loyal serpents spread outward like wings.

The past had led her here, and she wouldn't let this be the end.

Her feet curved around the branch where she crouched, focusing on balance, finding her physical precision.

"There are many I've killed," she said, voice an escaping hiss. "And there will be more."

Medusa released the trunk and leapt, bracing for an impact with Perseus and his shield. Branches slapped her as she descended, her heart pounding. Just a few seconds more and she would be upon him.

A strangled gasp erupted from him at the ensuing cacophony, and he whipped upright. His eyes flared, that blue pigment deepening with fright, as she locked gazes with him.

That was all it took.

The stonification started there, sweeping to his forehead, nose, cheeks.

She crashed onto the shield and rolled, wincing from the landing.

By the time she righted herself, Perseus had relinquished his flesh. His form was sprawled backward, collapsed on the leaf-strewn grown, limbs upraised, mouth hanging open in a silent shriek. She swayed, staring at the details of his cursed body, the angle of his nose and the pads of his fingers.

He was surrounded by natural detritus, his sword drawn uselessly, hair no longer golden but ashen gray.

The subject of her nightmares. How pathetic he now looked. How thoroughly she stole his power over her.

She spat at him, retrieved his shield, and left Perseus's remains in the shadows.

***

Her stomach stitched, a bump forming on her forehead from a branch. The snakes held themselves aloft, bouncing with each step, triumphant. She couldn't yet share their relief, not fully.

An evening glow seeped through the thick foliage and the heat decreased.

Please say Lee made it, she thought.

Medusa spotted the forest's edge and hurtled into the hills beyond. In the distance, she saw the dark silhouette of the shack against the skyline. There was no recent sign of activity, which was both distressing and reassuring. Perseus might have come with others and despite her earlier bravado, she wanted to avoid further killing that day.

The hills rolled beneath her feet as the ache in her abdomen continued. It was worse than having run too far. She feared it was a bruise from her descent in the tree, but there was no opportunity to linger on bruises.

She skidded to a halt as she approached, searching the doorframe and what was beyond.

"Lee!"

Urgently, she pressed against one of the crumbling walls, her gaze scouring the interior.

"Medusa?"

Lee lurched from behind a wall, his complexion pale.

"Are you hurt?" he asked, colliding with her.

"Lee! Yes, I mean no. I'm all right." She nearly choked, hands squeezing his limbs searching for any wounds. "And you?"

"I returned without incident." His brow furrowed. "Where is he?"

She hesitated only a moment before replying. "Dead."

"Good." His mouth turned to a grim line, holding her arms. "We should leave. I don't know if there was someone else with him…"

Dread rose in her throat, tasting of bile, and she shook herself. She couldn't collapse now. They had to go farther, to assure their safety.

To ensure any future at all.

"I will go wherever you do," he said. "I packed the blanket and the rest of the food I found."

She swiped at her moistening eyes, trying to stifle her tears. *He considered this, thought it through. He means to go with me.*

"Yes, we'll run," she said, believing him. "We can go to a cave I stayed in coming here. I stored extra supplies there…"

He made a soft sound of amusement. "Of course you did. You plan ahead better than anyone I have known."

She prickled briefly, fearing further criticism. But the softness of his eyes struck her, and the snakes nudged Medusa toward the empty doorframe. Beyond, dusk clutched at the landscape with frenzied fingers. The ball of tension relaxed.

"Then let's go," she said.

Their hands held fast as they left her temporary house. She glanced back once, awed by how the sunset cast the dilapidated structure in the hues of a dream. Her existence there leaned far more into the vein of terror, but at least she'd been able to share the latter part with Lee.

The swollen river appeared to their left, still as rambunctious as the previous day. They would have to cross it somewhere narrower. She panted, looked at him, and quickened their pace. Lee had no trouble matching, his gait an impressive stretch. Despite their weariness, they retraced their steps, plunging into the congealing night.

Chapter 10

Evening draped heavily, and with it an unseasonal chill. Stars sang silent chords of color and light, hiding behind small tufts of clouds that coasted by occasionally. The moon was just shy of full, outshining almost all other sparks in the sky, its bruises basked in soft purple. Her living crown crowded close to her scalp, their whispering tongues barely audible to her own ears.

Neither of them spoke, nor dared to breathe loudly into the enclosing quiet. They hurried together, paces matched, and she never loosened her grip on Lee's hand. She told herself it was for guiding him quickly. She knew it was more than that.

And by the warmth of his fingers twining with hers, she guessed his sentiment was similar.

She tried not to blink, for each time she did the flash of Perseus's shield—which thumped rhythmically on her back—struck, so too his form reflecting on the shiny surface. In the shadows of her lids, his frozen expression remained etched into her very flesh, and she understood his death wouldn't be forgotten. Like all that came before, each man who'd pursued her with the goal of destroying such a monster. Perseus was less afraid than most. He'd looked smug in each of her nightmares, a sense of righteousness that gave him a sinister glow. His existence was an invasion then and had continued for every night since.

That will change.

She jutted her chin, satisfaction stealing over her. She'd denied him the glory of dispatching her, a scourge on humanity, made by the gods and abandoned to her fate. Perseus the Hero would have summoned jubilant groups as he proclaimed his victory and held her severed head above, a gruesome trophy, his knuckles whitened from gripping the horde of dead snakes.

It would have been a harrowing tale indeed, but she had seized it as her own.

With a side-long glance, she surveyed Lee. She thanked her eyesight for the chance to see him, even in near darkness, for his profile caused her heart to clench, the line of his nose and curve of his lips their own landscape.

Perhaps he sensed her gaze. He stumbled and righted himself at once, swallowing the sound of a curse. She almost snorted a laugh, surprised by the levity he offered, and the last of her tension evaporated.

They'd survived. They would keep surviving.

She recognized a bend in the river from her previous trek. It was shallow and rocky, narrower than what they had observed. She squeezed Lee's forearm, slowing, fascinated by how his muscles worked beneath her touch.

Don't be foolish. Focus on escaping.

"On the left," she said, unnerved by her own voice after a couple of silent hours. "We can cross there."

He angled in her indicated direction. "The river does sound quieter."

"It's where I crossed before. The cave's farther to the east."

She stepped forward, but he caught her, tugging her back. "How are you doing?"

"What?" Her mind seemed to shutter. "I'm… I'm merely hungry."

"As am I. But I have a feeling, you know I meant more than that."

"Well…" She paused, fingers loose in his, and cleared her throat. "After what happened?"

"Yes, Medusa." His voice reminded her of moss, inviting her closer.

"I'm all right," she lied.

Her companions stiffened, and she willed him not to ask again. Not at that moment. The energy required to lie a second time exceeded her.

He seemed to understand and remained quiet, rubbing the skin between her forefinger and thumb, raking the ember in her stomach into a blaze.

"How are you?"

He squeezed her, his touch dispersing an intoxicating heat. "I've never been better, but I'm ready for that cave."

There was no jest in the first part of his claim. She allowed his meaning to infiltrate entirely, relishing the implications. Her toes sunk into the mud of the riverbed as they stood, but she couldn't ignore how she sagged with exhaustion.

"Here we go then," she whispered, resuming their approach, and lifted her collection bag high in the air to keep its inadequate contents dry.

With no reason to hesitate, they plunged into the water and pushed against the steady surge. Once in it, the flow was noticeably diminished, a small gift. There was little danger of drowning, but she still brought their joined hands to her chest. At some point, the need to keep him within a tangible range had blossomed incongruously. She wondered if the desire, so recently released from its apparent cage, would ever leave her entirely having grasped freedom.

Do I want it to? In ripples of enthusiasm, her tangle of serpents communicated their opinion. Lee tilted in their direction, a tentative smile forming. If they weren't in the middle of the river, she would stop, stare, surrender to the expression. No one had ever given her companions a smile.

She swallowed what felt like an oblong stone and focused on their crossing. The water churned, her thighs submerging as they passed the midpoint. Her attention stuck to an outcropping nearby, a glistening smear in the moonlight. His strides lengthened and suddenly Lee was at her side, no longer trailing behind, wading in tandem. She eyed him, hoping she wouldn't stumble in her surprise, and he angled his upper half in her direction.

"In case we get swept away. I'd rather we be close as possible."

Despite the cool air and colder water, her body heated. "I would too."

The river shallowed, signaling their arrival on the opposite bank.

"We're almost there," he said, his tone rising in the hint of a question.

She suppressed the chatter in her teeth and used a tall rock on the bank for stability. They scrambled from the flow using both hands, and an immense weight lifted off Medusa's mind. It wasn't a wall or an ocean. It was merely a river prone to flooding, but the dangers of her past were beginning to lose some of their sharpness with each fresh step.

Lee twisted the water from his clothes, inspiring her to do the same. Then they hurried onward, reaching a tucked away shadow within a massive rock that was big enough for two. They nestled in the enclosure, a sanctuary all their own.

***

The tree bark, harvested from a neighboring hilltop, was surprisingly supple. She chewed it wordlessly, relishing how he ate beside her, content and fulfilled. The fish Lee bagged from her house had survived the river crossing well enough, but she longed for more. A bruise formed on her ribs from the unfortunate collision with a tree branch the previous day, and Lee still boasted his array of scratches from his own violent encounters. But there could have been worse outcomes than that.

"Will there be more hunters?" His question arrived without warning.

She huddled beside him, knees raised to her chin. "There always are."

"Then you must find somewhere else. Somewhere they won't recognize or fear you."

He fiddled with an old leaf, slumped somewhat under the cave's ceiling, which was too low for him to stand.

The stories have spread so far, she thought. *Perhaps there is no such place.*

"And you? Will you return to the village?"

He balked at the suggestion. "Never... They believe I am bad luck."

"Oh. You remembered something?"

"Some." He exhaled, brow furrowing.

She didn't push, no matter how furiously her curiosity flared. A subtle wind whistled past the opening, and her snakes made similarly expectant sounds. When at last he spoke, it was halting.

"I made things... Tools and items to help the farm," Lee said, fitting two stones into his palm. "And I aimed to perceive more. There were... stars and wonders. I looked up and sought answers. That's why the gods stole my sight, I think. I dared to believe the heavens were vaster than we'd ever imagined."

Medusa went cold, understanding the true depths of their cruelty. "They stole your way of understanding."

"I don't know exactly who, but others witnessed," he continued, seemingly lost in the recollection, as if each detail unveiled itself gradually. "Everything was a blur in the moment. The god who took my eyes could have killed me. Or taken my mind for further punishment. But they decided I should live in darkness, to know fully mourn what I had lost."

The words splintered out of him. His entire form tensed, and before she could consider what she was doing, her arms encircled his shuddering limbs. She said nothing, rocking their bodies, moving against the onrushing grief. He burrowed deeper, holding her elbow, curling toward her chest.

"I miss the stars," he said, rasping from the arrival of tears. She nodded profusely, hoping that reassurance surpassed what her uncertain words couldn't possibly hold. Her swarm of serpents eased to him, lingering just beyond touching his head. Vision swimming, she remembered all that she was forced to leave behind, too. The joy of her sisters as they rowed the waves, the gifts her father had crafted when she was young, a future she hadn't yet defined.

The gods take everything.

But the anger didn't last, attention finding the man she held, the very individual who had accepted her twice over, and drew his chin upward. He trembled in response, heartbeat mirrored in her own chest. When the snakes crowded closer, he didn't flinch. Instead, his eyelids widened in apparent awe.

"They're not gone, the stars," she said, eyes searching his features. "Do you want me to describe them to you?"

His fingertips darted to her cheek, the pressure little more than her snakes's tongues.

"Please."

Courage strengthened her, and she leaned into his touch, bringing her lips there. Feelings chased the next as she noted the circumstance, the tangle of hope, excitement, anticipation, and impatience. By the racing of his pulse, she'd wager he shared the charging, rampant overwhelm. There was an irony present; that they had become a stone surrounded by the floodwaters of emotion. Her father had once spoken of such things, the flurry of adoration, but she never grasped his meaning until now.

She leaned into Lee, dragging her thumb over the swell of his earlobe, eliciting a sharp, breathy noise. She withdrew, fearing she'd gone too far, but he seized her, moisture gathered on his lids, tangling in his lashes. When she didn't resist, he brought her hand back to his cheek. The soft skin seemed more intimate than anything she could imagine. A thrilling exhale escaped him, not quite a moan nor a sigh. That novel and yet familiar burn of risk and hunger solidified as he cupped the base of her head.

"Medusa."

Briane Willis

Her name from his throat carried extra tones, depths, textures. She wanted him to say it again, wanted to hear it uttered for the rest of her life. His mouth was close enough to claim.

She couldn't manage uttering his in return, but another kind of response struck her with the force of the tide.

The halo of snakes chirped in encouragement, the last realization she had before kissing him.

Then, her senses filled with nothing else.

He tasted of trees, and sweet grass, smelled of nighttime. Curls tickled her forearms as they sunk deeper, torsos crashing at the embrace. Neither moved from the fierce initial impact, when holding meant more than exploring. But when they broke to inhale, a necessity more than a want, their prompt rejoining was of lightning in a crackling cloud.

They fumbled at first, noses bumping and bodies overlapping. She ached to track his skin as they kissed, desperate to map his specificity. What caused a greater hurdle was his own urgency to touch her. Clothes, as tattered and useless as they were, added a further barrier to their frenzy. She slid onto his lap, an impulse and motion wholly peculiar, too engrossed to consider her escaping moan.

On some later day, she would realize how her shame had long since evaporated in his presence.

He nipped at her lip, trailing kisses along her jaw, and she turned sinewy as the snakes. When she grabbed a fist of his shirt and kissed him deeper, a braid of thrill wove them tighter. In this, she devoured his reciprocating ribbon of passion, matching with the undulations in her own limbs.

They stayed enamored of the other until nearly dawn, before she remembered her promise to him.

Medusa ushered him as upright as he could be in the cave, and they drifted beyond to the ghost of sunrise. Several stars still glimmered, resisting night's end.

We, too, will resist, she thought.

Lee stepped into place on her left, turning his face skyward, lids shut. He draped one arm around her and she craned onto her toes to kiss him once more.

"I'll try to describe it, but words aren't my strength," Medusa said.

"Hearing your voice will be enough."

Her miasma of companions stilled. "Perhaps we find a place where the stars are different."

"We?"

She nudged him, affection lifting a hidden weight. "I thought that was obvious by now."

"Of course. Find a different sky, that way I won't be able to tell if you're not describing it quite right." He grinned, and she took a step back. Lines gathered in bunches around his eyes, angling out from his irises, the somber brown that couldn't decipher her own burgeoning smile. There had never been an expression so full of tenderness. She softened, accepting his jest, and rested her cheek on his shoulder.

"That would work for all of us," she said.

"To live beneath another sky, then." He folded her as close to his heart as was physically possible, as her snakes nestled into the heat permeating from them.

A place beyond gods and their punishment.

As day replaced night, Medusa recounted each disappearing splinter of star to Leandros, pressing them into his mind, rekindling memories and forging ones anew.

Epilogue

A form solidifies in the roiling surf, turbid against the white froth. Sharp words find her, and a threat. She shivers as the water reaches higher. It slips over her, and she sinks. There is nothing in her lungs, no escape. And Poseidon is still coming.

Medusa jolted awake, a cold sheen coating her skin. Her living companions seethed, some darting in search of an intruder, some crouching at her scalp. She eyed the darkened corners of their modest residence, but all appeared normal.

The kitchen existed in its usual midpoint between mess and cleanliness, with jars of smoked fish on a shelf next to the mushroom and berry bowls. A stringed instrument, worn by a pair of expert hands, sat on a chair. The front door was in its frame, so too the windows. On the wall hung a dead man's shield, dulled by time.

They'd been lucky to locate such an abode on a different continent, inhabited by a generous but insular community. The local inhabitants either didn't notice or declined to comment on Leandros's blindness, and Medusa kept her gaze averted and snakes covered with a shawl, a necessity she was resistant to at first. Eventually, however, Lee convinced her it wasn't because of dishonesty or shame, but a choice of safety.

Thankfully, their sinuous companions didn't mind.

Medusa and Lee maintained a respectful distance in gratitude, building their wooden house, cultivating a simple garden, and gathering enough fish to survive and leaving all else for their disparate neighbors.

Everything was in its proper place, including her and those she loved.

It's not real, she told herself, and the snakes believed it, sliding into the tapestry of contentment splayed around her.

On the bed, Leandros curled nearer, pressing into her pillow. She traced a finger down his temple, past his cheekbone, and along his jaw. He released a small sleepy sound and his lids fluttered open instinctively.

"Are you all right?"

She slipped back under the blanket, nestled beside him, and nodded into the crook of his neck.

Facing each other, she rooted her palm in his hair and withdrew a deep kiss from his parted lips.

He pulled away, worry lining his forehead. No matter how well she tried to cover them, he detected her feelings.

"It was that nightmare," he said.

"Yes. Only that."

"But it has been months since you've had one."

She chuckled, tracking the stretch of moonlight as it contoured his face. "Your memory is too good."

His expression lightened somewhat. "Perhaps losing it those years ago and regaining was a strength, but I am unwilling to give my near-drowning experience any credit for who I am now." He wrapped a leg under hers, snuggling closer.

"Maybe that too was from the gods, an apology for stealing your sight," she said. Too late she realized her tone shifted dark without intention.

He huffed. "Neither will I award their contribution. And yet..." He raised his hand and let her crown of serpents thread his fingers. "You all were such a gift. Thank you for helping keep Medusa safe, little ones."

Each creature darted and bobbed in response, tiny red tongues lapping at the cool air.

He hummed a song at them, their favorite melody, and she worried her heart would burst from a confounding, staggering joy flourishing in the space between them. She could dwell here, on the edge of land and sea, unknown to everyone else in the world, for whatever amount of eternity persisted.

Though she missed her father and sisters, she held her new family tighter than soil nurtured seeds.

"Will you tell me about tonight's sky?" he whispered, touching her side with his from shoulder to toes.

"Dawn is a long way off," she began, their routine comforting. "The darkness between the stars is lush enough to touch. Two stars flash the most like candles snuffed out and relit."

She grinned, knowing how she'd improved in her descriptions. How he had helped in that regard. She couldn't allow him to be the superior poet.

Her voice simmered lower, and by the heavy tilt of his head, she knew he was already on the brink of sleep.

Medusa stared at the sky, watching the shift of clouds. Lee's breath ebbed, a mimic of the waves just outside their home, as her snakes made a languid nest of ringlets. Morning would come, and another night, filled with song and the bubble of stew, the rush of pleasure in the body, and the luminance of devotion brighter than any eyes could perceive.

Acknowledgments

The same incredible support team that made my previous three publications this year possible once more buffeted me over the finish line. First and foremost, Dawn Adepoju, for your mind-boggling enthusiasm for the story and the spectacular art, I am exceedingly grateful!

Denise Broussard, a guiding light of fiction and inspiration, you are cherished. For each click I received on AO3, I thank you. The friends who read early drafts of this tale, I hugged you already and I will hug you again. To Chani Wells, such an early advocate, thank you for all your insight. Linda Gioja, may my words of appreciation and adoration never stop reaching you!

And I reserve all that remains, every piece that I hold together with my frazzled fingers, for the wondrous beings I call my partner and child. I love you very much.

Written in Leaves

Interested to read chapter one and the companion piece,
The Myth of the Kinnaree?
Sign up for Briane's newsletter at:
BrianeWillis.com

Mireille Morin lives a secluded life as the gardener of a popular teahouse in Paris. They straddle the line between man and woman, content in their own skin. But when a gentleman stumbles into their life, they are forced to analyze the true meaning of contentment.

Benjamin Antony Alden runs his family's publishing house with focus and passion. He publishes a variety of books unique to Paris and professional success follows. So too does loneliness. As he stumbles into the world of the gardener, he soon falls in more ways than one.

They embark on an unexpected arrangement and form a bond neither realized they had secretly been craving.

www.ingramcontent.com/pod-product-compliance
Lightning Source LLC
Chambersburg PA
CBHW070646130626
46555CB00006B/2726